P9-CFE-544

He'd shaken her trust in him.

Gina wasn't willing to tread a path that could collapse beneath her feet. And believing Toby's story was too big a hazard. He'd made her care about him. She wouldn't give him the power to break her, too.

"It's a nice story. Almost as touching as the one you wrote about the senator and the prayer journal. But I can't afford to believe you. Trust isn't part of a five-year plan. It's a commitment, a loyalty that lasts forever. And I'm a forever kind of girl. You're a short-term kind of guy. It was fun fighting with you, but then, it was all just a game to you, wasn't it? Congratulations, you win." She kept her eyes open against the cold sting of tears, knowing that if she blinked they'd escape, and then he'd know how much he'd almost won.

He reached out and cupped her cheek. "If I've won, then why does it feel like I'm losing my best friend?"

KD Fleming worked in a number of jobs before realizing she had the heart of a storyteller. She lives in west central Florida with her husband of sixteen years. They enjoy fishing, yard work and cheering on their favorite college team when not looking for snow in the Great Smoky Mountains or relaxing on the balcony of a cruise ship. KD loves reading and working with her three critique partners.

KD FLEMING

Her Hometown Reporter

HEARTSONG
PRESENTS

If you purchased this book without a cover you should be aware that this book is stolen property. It was reported as "unsold and destroyed" to the publisher, and neither the author nor the publisher has received any payment for this "stripped book."

Recycling programs
for this product may
not exist in your area.

LOVE INSPIRED BOOKS

ISBN-13: 978-0-373-48782-0

Her Hometown Reporter

Copyright © 2015 by Karen Fleming

All rights reserved. Except for use in any review, the reproduction or utilization of this work in whole or in part in any form by any electronic, mechanical or other means, now known or hereinafter invented, including xerography, photocopying and recording, or in any information storage or retrieval system, is forbidden without the written permission of the editorial office, Love Inspired Books, 233 Broadway, New York, NY 10279 U.S.A.

This is a work of fiction. Names, characters, places and incidents are either the product of the author's imagination or are used fictitiously, and any resemblance to actual persons, living or dead, business establishments, events or locales is entirely coincidental.

This edition published by arrangement with Love Inspired Books.

® and TM are trademarks of Love Inspired Books, used under license. Trademarks indicated with ® are registered in the United States Patent and Trademark Office, the Canadian Intellectual Property Office and in other countries.

www.Harlequin.com

Printed in U.S.A.

For I say, through the grace given to me, to everyone who is among you, not to think of himself more highly than he ought to think, but to think soberly, as God has dealt to each one a measure of faith.
—*Romans* 12:3

To my wonderful husband, Frank, for your faith in me to write the best book I can. You have the perfect shoulder for me to lean on. You are my heart.

To my critique partners—Carol Post, Sabrina Jarema and Dixie Taylor—thank you for your honest and priceless feedback. But most of all, for being my dear friends. You'll always be beyond compare to me.

To my wonderful agent, Nalini Akolekar, and my fabulous editor, Kathy Davis. Both of you inspire me to reach higher. I wouldn't be where I am today without either of you. You are both the greatest.

And thank you to Casting Crowns, my favorite band ever. The lyrics God gives you inspire and help me create characters that are true but broken in a way only God can fix.

Chapter 1

"Would you hold still for one minute?" Gina tugged hard on the two sides of his tie, steering him back in front of her. "You aren't walking through those doors as my guest with this pathetic attempt at a slipknot—which is crooked, no less. Didn't your daddy teach you how to tie a tie?"

Toby Hendricks cleared his throat and tried to stay as still as possible while his "friend" trussed him up tighter than a Sunday goose. It was just the recreation center attached to Grace Community Church, not the actual sanctuary. No need to feel any concern about earthquakes or collapsing roofs just because he was walking through the doors. But still, the noose around his neck cinched tighter as his throat thickened with unease. "My father was already at work by the time I got up for school in the mornings. And I only went to church when I came to visit my grandparents in the summer."

Her fingers paused. "I'm sorry. I guess I was projecting my family onto yours." She straightened his collar and brushed the slightly wrinkled fabric of his dress shirt smooth across his shoulders. "There. All done."

He offered his arm and she tangled hers with his before they started up the sidewalk to the main entrance. "So, how is it that you're a girl and you know how to tie a tie? Don't tell me you actually learned something from your brothers."

She didn't slow her pace or even toss one of her caramel curls in his face. No, Gina Lawson, the best connection a reporter could ask for to the most important people of Pemberly, Georgia, wasn't one to play coy. She was direct. Very direct. With quick fingers.

"Ow!" He snatched his arm free of hers and rubbed the stinging burn on the underside of his triceps muscle. "That had better not leave a mark."

"Trust me, it will." She grinned unrepentantly at him. "I simply watched while my dad taught my brothers how to tie their ties. You'd be surprised how many guy things I know how to do." She sauntered ahead of him, swinging her little purse around her finger by the gold chain that served as a strap.

So when they'd recently had their tug-of-war over the lug wrench and who was going to change her flat tire, she really had known what she was doing. Well, he'd been there, and he could loosen the lug nuts a lot faster than she could with her girl-muscles. But he knew better than to say anything like that.

She threw him a smirk over her shoulder. He beat

her to the door and held it open, ignoring the sparkle of mischief in her light cinnamon eyes as she walked past him, leaving a misty vapor of citrusy fragrance. Orange blossoms. How appropriate for the occasion.

Giving her a hard time was part of the fun of hanging around with Gina, even if he accompanied her in hopes of hearing something newsworthy. But she didn't feed him information, and he respected her for that. Her loyalty to her influential friends ran as deep as that to her family. He wasn't allowed to ask questions about any of them, personal, political or otherwise. Of course, he still did. And he'd improved the speed of his reflexes dramatically because of it.

But today he was dealing with a nervousness he'd never experienced before. Toby Hendricks, reporter extraordinaire, did not hang out in churches. Growing up caught between two divergent views about faith had left him wary. His grandparents were people of faith and attended church regularly, while his parents never darkened the door of a church.

They also had opposing views about people. His grandfather, Pops, helped others simply because they needed assistance. His father exerted himself to help others only if it benefited him in some way.

Gina was a lot like Pops in that regard. But in Toby's opinion, helping others just for the sake of helping was outdated. His dad had taught him to mingle with those who could help him get ahead in his career and elevate his social standing. Gina was that connection for him, and nothing more. But it was okay because they had an understanding. Gina didn't like to be the only one without a date, so she often asked Toby to accompany her to her many social events. It was a win-win—she had a date, and he might get a story.

Today was a special day twice over for Gina's friends. A belated wedding reception for Jeremy and Abby Walker combined with the dedication of Grace Community Church's new recreation center. Gina had been Abby's assistant on the project, helping ensure it came in on time. They were celebrating a lot today.

"Before we go into the main room, remember your promise to me." She twisted one of her curls around her finger.

"Yes, I got it the three times you reminded me on the way here. 'No interrogating the guests, don't pepper Pastor Walker with a million questions about why I can take his picture now and I couldn't before. No asking him and Abby Blackmon Walker why their wedding ceremony was so private but their reception is so public.' I got it. I'm still curious as to why, but I got it."

"Jeremy had just lost his parents. He loves Abby. And neither one of them wanted to wait to get married. And I don't blame him. I'd hate to be alone, too." She blinked several times quickly as if she had something in her eyes.

Gina was the least lonely person he knew. After all, she had five siblings. He shook his head. "You want me to believe that you don't find it strange that we never heard anything about the pastor's parents until they died. Then suddenly he gave me a private interview, giving credit to Abby for helping him overcome his fear of cameras. Now he can pose with her for enough photos to fill ten photo albums." He snatched his arm out of pinching range just in time.

Gina plopped her hands on her hips. "Be careful, Pinocchio. Your nose is growing and sticking itself into other people's business."

"I'm a reporter. It's my job to ask the tough questions. It's how I get the *real* story."

"Tough, not nosy? How would you like it if I grilled you about your family or interviewed the long list of women you go out with all the time, hmm? I can ask them what they think their prospects are of getting you to finally commit. I bet they'd jump at the chance to talk about the possibilities of marrying you."

He ignored the cold sweat breaking out on the back of his neck and flashed her a smile. "I would answer any questions you have about my family. And you know getting serious about someone doesn't fit into my career plans."

They stepped through the open double doors and into a massive room where the white concrete walls were hidden behind yards and yards of tulle in rose pink and matted gold. Balloons and streamers dangled from the tall ceiling. Potted palms created little alcoves with small tables and chairs for those looking to remain outside the main crush of people.

The room could easily hold a thousand people and looked as if it was that full at the moment. Toby checked his back pocket for his little notebook. A story could happen anywhere.

The second they cleared the doors, Gina was attacked by a small bundle of energy dressed in a caterer's black uniform with a snow-white apron covering her middle. "Oh, thank goodness. I really need your help." She panted for breath, her eyes darting a bit wildly around the room.

"Frannie, what's wrong?" Gina gripped the dark-haired tornado's hands, forcing her to make eye contact.

Ah, the older sister with the catering business.

"Paul and Mike called in sick with the stomach flu. I have Graham and Mia in the kitchen plating the hors d'oeuvres as quickly as they come out of the oven. But I need them out here serving the guests while I finish the display for the wedding cake." Her lips trembled and she scrunched up her forehead. Pools of moisture glistened in her dark brown eyes, but she fought it.

No way. Nope, nope, nope. He knew Gina would donate a kidney to a family member for no other reason than their blood connection. And she'd have him in the kitchen with burned fingers if he gave her the chance.

Well, she wasn't roping him into anything this time. "Uh, why don't you go help your sister? I'll just mingle." When she tried to protest, he motioned toward her sister. "I'll be fine. It isn't like I don't know everyone here."

Her gaze met his and she didn't return his smile. She didn't trust him. She didn't have to say it. The questioning look along with the twirling of that strand of hair around and around her finger said it all. "You promised." Her gaze held him captive.

"Yeah, I did. You may not like my methods, but you know I don't go back on my word."

After one last looping of her hair around her finger, she released it and him. "Go. But behave yourself."

As he wandered off to find someone to talk to he thought about their relationship. He liked Gina. More than he should. But she was too rooted to this small town with her big family and her close-knit friends to ever think of leaving. And he couldn't stay because he wanted more than the small town of Pemberly had to offer. He knew that Gina's family was always after her to find a good man. He wasn't that man. Not for Gina and not now. She was looking for forever no matter what she claimed.

Frannie yanked on her arm again. "Will you come on and stop mooning over that Clark Kent wannabe. He doesn't even have the right hair, or build, and he forgot to shave. Again."

Gina twisted in her sister's grasp. "Do you want my help or not?" At Frannie's nod she said, "All right. Then leave Toby alone. He needs to be here. I, apparently, need to be here so I can help you. And he gives me someone to talk to when everyone else is off being couples."

"Gigi says you can have any man you want. But you don't want one." Frannie shoved a bib apron at her.

Gina traded her sequined purse for an oven mitt and shook her head. She'd wanted to find Abby and see if the glow of true love was still painting everything roses or if Jeremy had been assaulted by one of the books in his office when he gave her some sass. Oh, well. There'd be time for mingling and laughing with her friends later. Her sister needed her now. So that's where she'd be.

"Gigi's right. I don't want a man right now. I'm here to help you. Give me something to do or I'm going back out there and being a guest."

That worked. Frannie blew a stray brown curl out

of her eyes. "I have to finish setting up the display around the wedding cake. Was it your idea to make the thing look like Cinderella's carriage?"

Gina grinned. "Yep. Don't you love it?"

"Love it? I'm the one who spent the whole afternoon measuring and cutting the dowels to the correct lengths. Making sure the glass stairway curves at the same angle from tier to tier. There's even a crystal pumpkin coach. Oh, no."

"What?"

"I saw two little boys eyeing the ceramic horses I left on the table. If they've taken them, I don't care who your friends are, I'll do the pat-down myself."

Gina grabbed her arm. "Take a deep breath. You've been running a catering business for five years. You're acting as if this is your first event. What's gotten into you?"

Frannie pulled away from her and repinned her hair, capturing the errant curl in the grip of the barrette. "My sister decided it wasn't any fun playing with the regular kids and had to go out and become best buddies with city councilmen, a whole flock of lawyers, a judge, a minister, and a United States senator. I heard someone say an NBA basketball player may drop in. Not to mention the US marshal who strolled through here earlier trying to snitch a crab puff off a waiting tray. This job is more important than any of my events in Atlanta because it's for your friends. If I mess up, what will your friends think of you—of me?"

Gina walked over and wrapped her arms around her protective sister. "They will think that your cooking is amazing, the cake is gorgeous and that accidents happen. They are people just like us. Don't downgrade the event to one of our dinners at home complete with food fights. Normal is fine. And they didn't hire you to cater this event just because you're my sister. They hired you because you're the best. And you're my sister. And I promised them a slight discount."

"You what?"

"Kidding. I offered and they refused. Both Katherine and Abby felt guilty asking you to do everything on short notice." She steered her sister toward the door. "Scram. Go save your horses, cowgirl. I have quiche, canapés, crab puffs, spanakopitas and latkes to plate."

Gina worked quickly. If she got ahead of Graham's and Mia's trips back for refills, she could peek out and see what Toby was doing. She could just kick herself for inviting him to come as her guest to *this* event just because he'd rescued her on the highway during a tornado warning. Toby had better not pepper Jeremy with questions about his parents' accident.

Jeremy was more comfortable with the media now, but he wasn't outgoing enough to ride on a float come Peach Blossom Parade Day, smiling and waving while every photographer in the county snapped his picture. She grinned. Unless Abby wanted him to, then he'd do just about anything.

Seeing her two friends get the guys God had picked out for them helped her keep believing He had one picked out for her, too. Just not right now. She worked at both women's offices and loved the challenge and the crazy schedule. When Abby's assistant decided to quit work when her maternity leave was up, it left Abby in the lurch. But since Gina was already bouncing between the two offices, and doing well at keeping both busy attorneys caught up on paperwork, they both offered her a huge raise and let her set her own hours.

Managing Katherine Delaney's office involved lots of paperwork but only a few phone calls because she was always in court or out on visits as the court-appointed advocate for some of the foster kids in the system. Abby was a contracts lawyer. She saw some clients, but most of her work involved an endless paperwork shuffle and countless calls and emails. Working for two lawyers handling vastly different areas of law kept Gina on her toes and gave her little time to get bored.

The stainless-steel double doors leading into the kitchen swung open as Gina put the last canapé on the tray. "Perfect timing." She came around to offer one of her younger siblings the next batch of hors d'oeuvres and stopped. "Oh, hi."

"Hello. Is it still considered perfect timing even though I'm not who you were expecting?" Shaun Fowler, former NBA superstar, offered her a smile worthy of a toothpaste commercial.

Just then, Mia whipped around Shaun and snatched the tray out of Gina's hand and was gone without saying a word.

She shook her head at her baby sister's actions, picked up a new tray and started filling it. "Couldn't be better. But aren't you supposed to be out there basking in the success of having your name etched into the boards on the basketball court?"

He had the decency to blush. "I didn't ask them to do that."

"Yeah, but you didn't beg them not to either." She grinned. To think she knew a celebrity well enough to banter with him. He was so cute. She was nuts. All that gorgeousness right in front of her and—no sparks. But she wasn't above a little flirting. After all, being around a guy like Shaun did a lot to lift a girl's spirits.

The six-foot-nine-inch former NBA All-Star slid his hands inside his pockets as he walked toward her, unaffected by her teasing accusation. She set the tray down before she dropped it. Abby, Jeremy, Katherine —even Katherine's husband, Nick, who liked to remain neutral in the opinion-giving department—had cautioned her about going out with Shaun. He was a player, on and off the court. But he was really nice. And totally gorgeous. When would a girl like her ever get to indulge her dream-date fantasy and go out with a man so far beyond her reach? It was too bad he was even less long-term-relationship-minded than Toby.

He leaned against the stainless-steel counter as she continued filling trays. His woodsy aftershave drifted over and tickled her nose. "How come you're in the kitchen? You should be out there celebrating a job well done along with the rest of us."

"And I would, except two of the caterer's main kitchen helpers came down with the flu and she was shorthanded."

Her brother and sister came in and grabbed the loaded trays, dropping off their empties. She pulled a cookie sheet out of the oven and put another in to heat, then started arranging canapés on a fresh tray.

"She should have hired more staff to make sure she

was covered for an event like this." He reached down and took one of the Brie-and-Black-Forest-ham rolls waiting to be plated and popped it into his mouth. He chewed slowly before swallowing, never taking his eyes off her. "Although she does amazing things with spices. Maybe you should just threaten to never use her again."

The heat that had started in her chest as the flush of a girlish infatuation was singeing its way up to the lower part of her neck and higher until her ears smoldered and her cheeks tingled with quiet fury. "For your information—"

"Gina, babe. I thought you said you were only going to be a few minutes. Abby and Katherine are waiting for you." Toby ambled into the room and stopped beside her.

Shaun pushed away from the counter until he was at his full height. She wasn't sure, but he might have even arched up on his toes a little. Ridiculous. He was already almost too tall to clear the door. And why would he preen in front of Toby anyway?

Toby stood there at six feet if he maintained perfect posture, with his three-day-old scruff of a beard and tousled sandy hair that was in dire need of a trim. Did Shaun see him as competition? For her?

Oh, please. She was not one of Shaun Fowler's conquests. Besides, he had insulted her sister. Nobody messed with her siblings but her. She blew out a heated breath, trying to ease her temper and gain some patience. "Shaun, the reason I'm in the kitchen is the caterer is my sister. She can't control when someone gets sick. If she could, she'd be working with a pharmaceutical company reproducing the cure-all as fast as they could make a batch. So don't criticize her management skills. She's very good at what she does. And she did call in a relief team. My younger brother, sister and me. We've all worked for her before. Her food is fabulous and her service and reliability are impeccable."

Toby angled himself nearer to her and rested his hand against the small of her back. The heat of his palm spread through her, soothing her and cooling her temper without him saying a word. Maybe he did have some special abilities like Superman. But enough of that. She was standing in the new recreation center's kitchen chewing out the most famous person she'd ever met while receiving moral support from the least likely man to give it in all of Pemberly. She led an ironic life.

"Shaun, I don't think you've met Toby Hendricks. He's a features reporter for the *Pemberly Sentinel*."

Toby's hand shot out in the time-honored tradition. She just hoped Shaun didn't crush his typing fingers, but then Toby only used his two index fingers. She shivered at the thought of how long it must take him to type his stories using that method.

"Nice to meet you. I was kind of surprised you didn't call me for an interview while all the construction was going on."

"Well, anything I needed to know about the project I was able to get from Mrs. Walker or Gina. They had all the details. You were just the money-man."

"Toby." Gina gasped before turning to face him. "That is a horrible thing to say." Then she looked at Shaun. "You'll have to forgive him. He hasn't mastered basic manners. I'm trying to teach him, but he's a very slow learner. We've gone over how to tie his shoes for weeks now."

Her sister came in and Gina handed her a filled tray, then went back to filling yet another, all the while keeping an eye on the two men vying for domination in the kitchen.

Shaun's eyes drifted toward the floor and Toby's feet, which were encased in dress shoes. "Hmm."

She set a full tray of canapés on the counter before patting Toby's arm. "Poor thing, he was so ashamed, he started wearing shoes that don't require tying. But we're all proud of him for recognizing his weakness and finding a way around it."

Shaun's laugh echoed around the room, reverberating through the stainless-steel counters and bouncing off the walls. "And I thought Abby was the one to look out for. Your snarkiness is razor sharp." His eyes turned a shade darker and his voice a tone lower. "I like danger."

Toby cleared his throat. "Gina, I wasn't kidding." His words and the impatience in his tone pulled her attention away from Shaun and his blatant flirting before she could respond. "Katherine and Abby want you out there. Tell me what you need done in here and I'll cover for you. Frannie said she'll be finished arranging the cake table in a few minutes."

She hesitated a moment before pulling the neck loop of her apron over her head and sliding it over his. "Right. I had better go, then. Who knows? They might be planning to throw the bouquet. With both of them out of the competition, I can take out the rest of those single women with a well-aimed elbow jab.

Come on, Shaun. I'll help you find your way back to the famous people."

He looked between Toby and her, but Toby had turned and reached for the oven door. It was a dismissal as plain as the words "get out."

Chapter 2

It was midafternoon and the reception for the Walkers' wedding and the grand opening of the recreation center was over. After Gina settled into her seat in the truck, Toby slammed the door shut. Once he was in, he slammed his, too. He couldn't get them away from here or her home fast enough. He jammed the key in the ignition and shoved the shifter into Reverse while tugging the silk knot of his tie loose.

"Do you mind letting me in on why you're so mad?"

He glanced over at her before checking his clearance of the car behind him as he backed out of the parking space. "Why would I be angry?"

"I don't know. That's why I'm asking you what put a bee in your bonnet?"

He brought the truck to a screeching halt. "A bee in my bonnet?" He shook his head, gripping the steering wheel until his knuckles ached. "You told an NBA All-Star I'm too stupid to tie my shoes. Could you have said anything to make me look more like an idiot than that? I know you think the sun rises and sets on Shaun Fowler, but you don't know what type of guy he is."

"Oh, really. I've worked with him for the past six months on the recreation project, going to dinner, meeting in his office and speaking to him on the phone. I think I know a little bit more about the man than you do."

"No, you don't. He was nice to you because of Abby. He was interested in her and thought cozying up to you was his ticket to a chance with her. He was using you, Gina."

She wrestled her seat belt off and grabbed for the door handle but turned back to face him before she opened the door. "You're right. If anyone could spot a parasite, it would be you. Because that's how you try to get your leads, isn't it? Tell me, did you chat with Nick and Jeremy long enough to get some juicy details for your next big newspaper story? I saw you with them and then I saw you huddled in the corner with your phone, your thumbs flying over your keyboard." She opened the door and got out.

Great. Another reason not to get serious about anyone. Temperament. And Gina's was beyond feisty. He set the parking brake with a sharp yank, then threw open his door and went after her. "Gina, wait. Gina."

She was a row of spaces ahead of him, her thin stiletto heels stabbing at the asphalt beneath her feet as she stalked back toward the entrance to the building.

Blowing out a long sigh, he jogged after her, catching her before she reached the glass door. He slapped his hand against the metal frame, holding it closed.

"Move."

"No."

She turned her head and met his gaze with eyes that had lost their usual cinnamon color and changed into a deeper, hotter red—like cayenne pepper. "If you don't take your hand off that door, you will limp home from here with a mark on you that I can assure you will be permanent and require stitches." She didn't blink. In fact, she didn't move anything but her lips as she uttered her promise.

He took his hand off the door. "I didn't mean what I said the way you took it. I just don't think you have that much in common with him. Anytime I saw him, he was always making eyes at Abby if she was nearby. And it's his loss. You'd make a great addition to one of those NBA-wives-and-girlfriends reality shows. Come on, do you think I'd be stupid enough to insult someone I'm beginning to believe knows how to maim without leaving a mark on the body?"

Her lips twitched, but he could tell she was fighting it. "What you said wasn't nice. I know you only hang around because you're looking for your next big story. Other men *are* attracted to me for more than who my friends are. I'm great girlfriend material. Not for you, of course. I have no interest in dating you. But other, more appealing men. I just don't have time to go looking for any of them right now."

He hadn't expected Gina to be defensive about herself. It wasn't something he'd ever encountered before. And he wasn't so sure he liked it either. He kept his mouth closed until he figured out what to say that wouldn't have her peeling off one of those incredibly high and spiky heels and using it to poke his eye out. After a moment or two of silence, he managed, "So, are you going to let me drive you home or are we going to stand here while the motor's running, waiting until it runs out of gas?"

"Jerk." She spun around and headed back in the direction of his truck.

"Ah, that's what every man longs to hear, you gorgeous sweet-talker you." He ambled along behind her, rethinking his original plan to invite her to the paper's Christmas party next weekend. Too much time with Gina always led to arguments.

She didn't speak to him for the entire ride across town to her apartment. It wasn't as if the silent treatment bothered him. Silence was golden in his book. But for Gina to remain silent for the fifteen-minute drive was impressive. He just hadn't thought she could keep her teeth clamped closed for that long. Never mind the gnashing and grinding sounds coming from her side of the truck. But she'd get over it. When he pulled up, she hopped out before he could turn the engine off.

"Enjoy the rest of your day."

She didn't turn around to wave or even make a face. Yep, she was not happy with him. And it wasn't anything new. Toby headed for home, and though he wanted to think about something else—in fact, anything—his mind kept coming back to Gina. He could read her like a book. No complexities. Simple and direct. She was open and warm to everyone. She was pretty easy to understand.

What he couldn't figure out was her close friendship with Abby Walker and Katherine Delaney. Gina and her two bosses came from very different backgrounds, and yet they were true friends. Men didn't operate that way. The more varied the background, the higher the level of competition between them. But with these women, it all clicked into place as if they'd known each other all their lives. Weird, but in a good way, he guessed.

Abby and Katherine were a complete contradiction. Katherine was a former foster kid who could have beaten Nick Delaney out of his city council seat but had traded him the seat for a wedding ring. And Abby Walker—now there was an incongruent bonding for sure. A successful contracts attorney who was also the daughter of a US senator was now married to Pemberly's favorite minister. He wouldn't have pegged Abby as a minister's wife, but she'd settled into her role as if born to it. And if the constant, fatuous smile on Jeremy's face was any indication, then they were made for each other. Crazy. They were all crazy.

Gina was the most logical of the three women. She didn't need grand gestures when he misspoke or forgot he had asked her to go to a movie with him because it was his weekend to write the movie-review column for Monday's paper and the big box-office hit was a romantic comedy. She'd laugh it off when he called and then tell him he owed her a steak or something. She never yelled or threw things. But if he was within reach when her temper soared, he was lucky a bruise was all he got if he reacted too slowly. Maybe he should avoid women who had lots of brothers.

Now, with her two best friends married, her family had to be closing ranks, sorting through the phone book or the church directory, or both, on the hunt for just the right man for her. Well, good luck with that infinite quest. Marriage wasn't what all those chick-flick movies and romance novels made it out to be. It was about at least one person giving up their dreams and, over time, growing to resent what they sacrificed for "love." That's how his father said it went. And with the chilly silences around his family's dinner table back when he was a teenager, his dad was obviously right.

Toby slept better at night knowing he'd never be naive enough to fall in love. To find himself roped into marriage. Real love meant the possibility of being hurt. His grandfather was a perfect example. Losing Grams had about done Pops in. Toby never wanted to give someone that kind of power over him or feel that much pain.

He had a plan and when the scheduled time came, he'd pick out the right woman and they would be a perfect couple, complementing each other's strengths and earning each other's respect. That's what marriage was about. It should be like a business deal, without all those emotions and romantic ideas so many women expected. Each spouse should appreciate what the other brought to the marriage that helped make the two a stronger unit.

Gina, with her perkiness and sassy attitude, wouldn't give anything up to offer support to the man in her life, he was sure of it. All the attention she received from her big family had given her the desire to compete, the need to always best her opponent. He didn't want to have to arm-wrestle his wife for the right to make the decisions for his family. He was the man. It was his job. Wasn't it?

After Toby dropped her off at her apartment, Gina had needed a shower. The steam and heavy odor of spices permeating the air in the kitchen while she'd pulled her rescue shift for Frannie had left her smelling like a Friday-night international buffet.

With her hair washed and towel-dried, she twisted it up and clipped it into place. Dressed in her usual Saturday-afternoon outfit of jeans, boots and a long-sleeved T-shirt, she grabbed her sweater on her way out the door. And caught the triple-locking hulk of wood just before it shut with her keys and purse still inside. In a blur, she rushed down the stairs of the apartment building and out to her car. Her grandmother would worry if she was late for her visit to the retirement villas.

She smiled at the nursing staff manning the reception desk as she hurried by on her way to the solarium. At the threshold of the doorway, she paused. Gigi sat across from Mr. Tobias with an oversized checkerboard between them. They were staunch competitors, not above causing a distraction if it gained one of them the upper hand in the match.

From the frown lines marring Gigi's forehead, Mr. Tobias was holding his own today. Gina walked into the room quietly, giving them time to find a stopping point if not the opportunity for one to declare victory. Just as Gina reached the small sofa where her grandmother was sitting, Mr. Tobias pounded his fist on the table and the checkers jumped and scattered off their squares.

"Tobias, you did that on purpose. I was about to make my move. You sabotaged the game. I win by default."

"I could have made it to Atlanta and back, on foot, by the time you made your move. But I'll get you next time. A little advice Genevieve, if you're going to take a man down, do it quick and spare him the pain."

Gigi huffed, then looked up and smiled. "Gina, darling. Come sit here and tell Gigi how the big party went today." She cast a stern glance at Mr. Tobias. "Don't mind him. His grandson stood him up today and he's pouting."

"Oh, Mr. Tobias. I'm sorry. He isn't sick, is he?"

"That scamp? No, he's probably out trying to be Superman again. What I wouldn't give to see the day when he runs into his green kryptonite."

Gina opened and closed her mouth, struggling for something to say in reply. Was he serious or teasing? "Well, I'm not sure there's much kryptonite around here."

Mr. Tobias laughed and moved the game table to the side so she could sit beside her grandmother. "That boy's kryptonite is women. Now, don't get me wrong, he doesn't disrespect them or do things he shouldn't. He has big plans for his future and settling down with the woman God has set aside for him isn't on his schedule just yet. But I keep telling him he needs to ask God what His plans are for him, otherwise he'll be fighting a battle up the hill all the way. And when he gets to the top, it won't be anything like he thought it would be, nor the best he could have had either."

"That's good advice. I know someone a lot like that. He's years away from thinking about a family yet he has loads of dating advice for me."

He smiled at her. "The only dating advice anyone needs to give you is how to shake off the admirers flocking to your door." He shot her a wink and a dimple of a smile.

Her cheeks heated more with embarrassment over the fact that there weren't any admirers beating on her door than with an old man's innocent flirting. "I think I'm safe for now."

Gigi caressed the leather cover of the heavy Bible she'd brought from her apartment. "Do you have time to read to us today?"

"Of course. Gigi, I told you I'd be late. I'm later than I expected because I had to help Frannie clean up."

"What? She has staff to do that. She doesn't need to be roping you into a weekend job to go along with all those hours you work during the week."

She reached out and stilled her grandmother's restless hands where she wove her linen handkerchief through her fingers. "Gigi, her main prep team came down with a stomach bug and couldn't make it. She didn't have time to find someone else. Besides, Graham and Mia were already there as servers. It would have taken too long to have them load the trays themselves before going out to serve the guests. I was happy to help."

"What about your date? I'm sure he wasn't happy sitting in the kitchen watching you rush from the oven to the counter."

"He was fine. He knew most of the people there so he mingled and ate way too much spanakopita."

They laughed and Gina opened the Bible. She glanced toward the glass walls of the solarium. "It was raining when I got here. If it gets any colder, we might have ice and sleet. I think winter is finally catching up to us."

Gigi repositioned her shawl closer around her shoulders.

"Did y'all want me to start with Psalm 23 or did you have something else in mind?"

Mr. Tobias moved over to the recliner next to the sofa beside Gigi. After he was settled in with the chair semi-reclined, he looked out at the rain that was becoming more solid and icy as it fell. "Since the weather's turned more to the season, how about reading from Luke about the story of Jesus's birth."

The solarium was decked in evergreen swags draped along the top of the glass walls. Red, gold and silver ribbons adorned huge painted glass orbs that glinted in the light, casting prisms of color along the ceiling. The Christmas story would be the perfect read, serving as a warm reminder of the greatest gift of all—God's love for humanity in the form of His son, Jesus.

She read the verses, taking her time, opening her heart and her soul to the worries Mary and Joseph might have faced on their journey. The story always humbled her, reminding her to give thanks. A gift was special because of the love the giver had for the one receiving it.

The clack of Gigi's knitting needles stopped when Gina closed the Bible. Mr. Tobias was snuffling softly with his head tilted to the side. His face was relaxed, without worry lines. Gigi moved her knitting bag aside and scooted closer to Gina, away from the sleeping Mr. Tobias.

"Gina, do you think George and Jenna would mind if I bring Mr. Tobias as my guest for Christmas?"

Gina kept her voice low. "Of course not. They'd love to have him. You know that."

Gigi was twisting the ends of her shawl around her fingers. Gina put her arm around the slender shoulders of her maternal grandmother. "Gigi, what's the matter?"

Gigi cast a glance at the sleeping man, then faced Gina, taking her hands in hers. "He is a dear, sweet man. He means a lot to me. We've kept each other from feeling lonely here. You don't know what it's like to be in a room full of people and look around knowing there's no one there just for you. Especially if you've had someone there for you before. I miss your papa so much, but Mr. Tobias and I have a special friendship."

Here it was almost Christmastime and both her best friends would be celebrating the season of love with their new husbands, and now even her grandmother had found a special friend. Gina knew exactly what it was like to be alone in a room full of people. She lived it every holiday when her sisters brought their boyfriends and her brothers braved the expectations that always followed when one brought a girlfriend to a big family gathering.

She was beyond pitiful, begrudging her grandmother the companionship and love of a kind man. She didn't really begrudge her that, but maybe she was a little jealous of the happiness, the tenderness, she witnessed between the two of them as they held hands on the walks they took around the lake or how he always held the door for her.

Those were the things Gina wanted. But enough was enough. She didn't have a man and Gigi did. She would do what she could to show her support for their relationship and let the family know they cared for each other.

"I'll talk to Momma and she'll let Daddy know. Everything will be fine. Everyone has met him and we visit with him when we come to see you. Besides, it isn't as if you've grabbed some stranger off the street to bring with you to dinner. But what about his family? His grandson. Don't they want him to be with them?"

Gigi was back to twisting the ends of her shawl, trying to find a way to explain something that obviously made her uncomfortable or unhappy.

"Gigi, it's okay. If he wants to be with you for Christmas, I'll make sure you each have a room. And if he wants to visit with his family, you and I can take him wherever he wants to go. Will that work?"

Gigi wrapped her is a strong hug. "Thank you, sweetie. He didn't want me to ask, but I told him you liked him and not just because he's my friend. He's your friend, too, isn't he?"

Gina smiled and gave her grandmother a soft kiss on the cheek. "Yes, I like him and yes, he's my friend. We'll make this the happiest Christmas he's had in a long time."

As she settled in for a long visit with Gigi, Gina couldn't help but wonder about Mr. Tobias's grandson. She wanted to share as many Christmases with Gigi as she possibly could. Why wouldn't he want to be with his grandfather? Was their family not close?

From Mr. Tobias's description, he sounded like a pretty nice guy. Maybe she shouldn't judge him before the fact. But it made her curious. And made her want to meet him. Maybe he was better marriage material than Toby Hendricks.

Chapter 3

Toby lounged in the chair in front of his boss's desk with his feet propped on the corner of the hunk of scarred wood. His hair shielded his eyes from the overhead fluorescent glare. He lowered his heavy lids down over his eyes. He'd give himself a few minutes to catch up on the sleep he'd missed last night.

After his fight with Gina outside the recreation center, he'd dropped her off at her apartment complex, then driven back across town to his studio apartment for some solitude. His phone had been ringing when he'd unlocked the door.

The second he answered, his father had begun screaming in his ear that Christmas was off. Pops wasn't coming because he wanted to be with his new lady friend. Toby had gotten off the phone as quickly as he could. No one else seemed to dread the holidays the way he did.

So now here he was, in Ivan the Terrible's office awaiting his story assignments. Somehow, they always included veiled orders to find some kind of dirt on Senator Blackmon. Toby had explained there wasn't any to be found, but Ivan wouldn't listen. He'd lean back in his oversized leather chair and run his tongue across his gold tooth.

Toby was waiting for the day he tried to make him create some of his own dirt to use against the man. That would be the day Toby found another job. He already spent more time with Gina than he was comfortable doing, per his boss's orders.

Ivan was also convinced there was a scandal behind Edward Delaney's past and his new daughter-in-law, Katherine. The craziness didn't stop there. He'd peppered Toby with a ton of wacko questions when he turned in the story he'd written from his interview with Pastor Walker right after the death of his parents. But as far as Toby could tell, they were all just regular people. No skeletons in their closets.

Ivan claimed there was more, though. Said he could feel it in his teeth—and sucked on that gold tooth again. The almost maniacal gleam Ivan got in his eyes when he talked about how to get the goods on the statesman creeped Toby out sometimes. He didn't want any part of it. His dream was to be recognized for his skill in uncovering the truth, not for bringing down those who helped the people of the community. He wasn't into yellow journalism.

Yeah, Toby wanted to get ahead in his career and had a reputation for following a lead as far as possible, no matter what. Once or twice, he'd even tried to head off another reporter to get there first. But his stories were the truth. They could stand up to the toughest scrutiny. Gina was only half-right about him doing anything for a story. He'd do anything to get the *real* story.

"Hendricks, you can sleep on your own time. We work around the clock here."

Toby pulled his feet off the desk and scooted up in the chair. "Well, aren't you chipper this morning."

The other man mumbled something while his back was turned, pouring himself a cup of sludge from a coffeemaker probably older than one of Gina's nephews. "Want some?"

He pushed his hair out of his eyes and shook his head. "I'm good. I have some juice in the fridge for later. So, what evil little plot have you thought up as my next assignment?" Toby chuckled.

Ivan didn't. Instead, he shuffled some papers around on his desk until his hand landed on the remote for the plasma TV mounted on the wall. He pressed a button and the screen came to life. On it was news footage of a press conference. Senator Blackmon was seated in the front row on the platform, left of the speaker's back, in full view of the camera.

Ivan kept it on mute. Toby watched the senator, somehow knowing that was the point of this visual aid. A couple of seconds later, Senator Blackmon reached inside his coat and pulled out a small book. He wrote something down, then slid it back into his pocket.

"See that?" Ivan jabbed a finger at the paused image of the senator in mid-motion on the screen. "Hendricks, did you see what he did?"

"Yeah, Ivan. He wrote something in a notebook. When did that become a crime?"

Ivan growled and pressed another button on the control he was aiming at the screen like a weapon. "Watch this."

"It would help if you told me what I'm supposed to be watching."

Just then, the camera panned the senate floor and he caught sight of Senator Blackmon in a different suit. He shook hands with the man he had been speaking to and as he started to walk away, he reached inside his jacket and pulled out the notebook. He stopped moving just long enough to scribble something inside before slipping it and the pen back into his pocket.

"See, he did it again. I'm telling you, that book has his secrets. He keeps it on him at all times. He never pulls it out while he's talking to anyone. He waits until after they're gone. He has to be taking notes on their conversations so he can use the information later."

"You don't know that. Maybe he has a bad memory and when he thinks of something he has to write it down or he'll forget."

Toby wasn't sure, but he thought Ivan muttered something colorfully unpleasant. "I don't understand what you want me to do. Whatever he's written down in there is private. It may not have anything to do with his position in the senate. And if it doesn't, it isn't my concern."

"Oh, yes it is. I'm making it your concern. I've let you run your feel-good stories about your little girlfriend's influential friends as big features on prime circulation days. You owe me, Hendricks. And it's time to pay the piper. I want that book."

"What? Are you crazy? And you run those articles as features because they sell papers. Ivan, think about what you're saying." Toby fought the icy dread filling his stomach. Surely, the man didn't expect him to—

"Hendricks." Ivan placed his meaty fists on his desk and leaned toward Toby. His squinted glare locked onto him. "I want that book and you're going to do whatever it takes to get it for me. If you don't, good luck finding another newspaper job anywhere in the Southeast."

Acid gurgled in his throat and he swallowed against the sting. "I wouldn't have a clue about how to get close enough to him to even ask him about the thing, let alone touch it."

"You aren't going to ask him for it. You're going to take it. If you can't bring it to me, then I want the contents. Take pictures, copy his notes into one of your little books. It doesn't matter how you do it. I. Want. That. Book."

"You're insane." Toby took a step back from the desk.

Ivan's eyes had gone wide and his grin too broad. The fluorescent light flashed off his gold tooth. "I'm determined. I've waited years for the opportunity to ruin that man. He thinks because he's a representative of the people, he's above the law. Well, he's going to learn just how mighty the pen can be in the right hands."

"Ivan, I'm not breaking the law for you and I'm not going to head a smear campaign against Senator Blackmon. I'm friends—just friends—with Gina and through her I have a somewhat close acquaintance with his daughter Abby, her husband and their friends."

"You'll do it or the next article that runs in this paper with your name in the byline will be so filled with plagiarized sentences, you'll be lucky to find a job selling newspapers from a corner newsstand."

"You can't—"

"You enjoy flitting around with that little brunette. You didn't act too guilty over stringing her along when I told you to use her for easy access to the political powers in this town. And it worked. But now it's time you earned one of your stories. I'll even let you write the piece. Just as long as you drive Senator Harold Blackmon to his knees." He brought his finger up and rubbed his tooth again.

Sweat dampened the middle of Toby's back. "Think about the integrity of the paper. Do you want the *Sentinel* sued, and rightfully so, for invasion of privacy, theft and I don't know what else we'd be doing that's against the law? He's chummy with a US marshal. Dekker. He was at Saturday's dedication. We'll get caught. I'll go to jail. This isn't right. I won't do it."

"You'll do it or you won't have a job. Take the afternoon. Spend some time counting up how much your soul is worth. But understand that if you come through those doors in the morning, I expect that book or a list of its contents in my hand by January 4."

"Gina would never speak to me again."

"Then go cry to her and see if she'll help you find somewhere to sleep until you can get a job that pays better than flipping burgers. Because if you don't deliver, you're through in the newspaper business. I'll see to that."

"Do you really hate him that much? You'd risk my integrity, the paper's and yours just to take him down." Toby shook his head in dazed confusion. "What did the senator ever do to you?"

"That doesn't matter. Let's just say I owe him this—and more."

Toby staggered from Ivan the Insane's office and dropped into the chair at his cubicle. He rubbed his hands over his face and up through his hair. What was he going to do? The feverish glint in Ivan's eyes made Toby believe he meant every threat he'd made.

But why?

He opened his desk drawer and grabbed his phone and a notebook. Palm-size, the same size as the one the senator had used.

After watching those news clips, flashes of memory popped into Toby's head. He'd seen the senator with the little book before. He kept it in the left breast pocket of his suit jacket.

Now that he knew about it, he was curious. But not enough to steal the book from the man. As the old cliché went, curiosity killed the cat, and Toby didn't have any plans on dying right now.

And just how was he supposed to get close enough to the senator to possibly touch the book, much less take it?

He had to get out of here. He needed to talk to someone. But who? Who would believe him even if he could tell them his boss had gone nuts and was coercing him to steal something from a US senator?

Anyone who might be able to help him knew the senator. Oh, man, he was going to end up in jail or on the street.

Gina. How would he ever look her in the eye again? She trusted him. Well, not totally, but when he gave her his word, she believed him. If he even considered doing part of what Ivan wanted, he'd be betraying his friendship with her. She would never forgive him. Gina was the most loyal person he knew.

He took the stairs down to the parking garage, then climbed into his truck. He backed out and exited onto Blackmon Street, the main road through downtown. Even the road's name taunted him with Ivan's demand. He'd never felt so lost, so confused in his life. Gina would urge him to pray, but he didn't know how.

There had to be someone—someone bigger than he—who knew what the right choice was. He could go to Pops, but Pops would badger the entire ugly story out of him. The only thing worse than the thought of Gina turning from him in disgust was breaking his grandfather's heart. He wouldn't be able to live with himself if he did that to Pops.

Grace Community Church came into sight up ahead. He didn't even know if churches left their doors unlocked so people could go inside and pray whenever they needed to. Was praying just for Sundays and before meals? He didn't know much about it, but he was desperate.

He parked near the recreation center. Maybe if he went in through the back door it wouldn't be as hard. He got out of the truck and walked up to the entrance he and Gina had used after the reception. The door came open when he pulled on it. This was a good sign. He stood just inside the doorway, breathing deep, acclimating his body to the air—holy air. This was part of the church, too, wasn't it?

He heard the steady drum of quick footsteps and a rhythmic thud followed by the *swoosh* of a net. He smiled for the first time that day. The pastor must be getting in some practice. He walked toward the double glass doors. Jeremy was inside, alone. *Thank You, Lord.* He hadn't realized he'd been praying, but he was definitely thankful for the quick answer.

Jeremy came down after another slam dunk. The ball shot toward Toby. He bent and picked it up, then tossed it back. "You've got pretty good game for a minister."

He grinned and wiped his sweaty forehead against the sleeve of his shirt. "Is that going to be the big headline for tomorrow's paper?"

The smile on Toby's face slid off. "No, they'd run that in the sports section."

"Something tells me you aren't here as a reporter."

Toby froze. "How—"

"A lot of ways. The main one is that I could tell how uncomfortable you were when we referred to the center as part of the church on Saturday. You were tugging at your tie as if it were a hangman's noose. And right now, you don't look afraid of your surroundings. You look like a man seeking refuge. One who sees this as the safest place he could be."

"Wow. No wonder everyone thinks you're the next best thing to God."

"Oh, no. None of that. I'm a man trying to do what God called me to do. I'm just like you except my boss's office is on a much higher floor and the retirement plan goes on forever."

Talking to the pastor broke him out in a cold sweat that held his shirt to his skin. He felt as if he were standing on a tightrope a hundred feet in the air with no safety net. "How does the privacy thing work with you? I mean, if I tell you something, you can't tell the police or that marshal, right?"

"That isn't what I was expecting you to ask, but I can work with it. Yeah, unless someone's life is in danger because of what you tell me, I can't reveal to anyone what you've told me in confidence without your permission. Even Dekker."

"Who?"

"The marshal."

"You know him?"

"I thought we were dealing with your problem right now."

"Yeah, right. My problem. Do I pay you?"

"For what?"

"For counseling."

"No." Jeremy was shaking his head and looking at him as if he'd lost his mind. "My counsel is free of charge. Although it'd be nice to see you sitting in the sanctuary during services on Sunday mornings."

"If you can help me with this problem, I'll sit in the front row."

"Then let's head back to my office. Something tells me we're going to need more privacy than we'll get in here."

Toby followed him. He still wasn't sure how much or what he would tell Jeremy. But the cold fingers of dread weren't squeezing his insides as hard. He could breathe. And a spark of warmth was growing in his chest, melting away some of the cold fear. He didn't have to do this alone. He let out a long sigh of relief.

In Jeremy's office, the pastor motioned Toby to the chair facing his desk. He pulled two bottled waters out of a small refrigerator and offered one to Toby.

"Thanks." He unscrewed the cap and took a long swallow.

"Sometimes the best way to do this is to just blurt it out. We can go back and pick it apart afterward, taking it one piece at a time. But the most important thing is that you get it out so we can both deal with it. It doesn't matter how you do it."

Toby inhaled a long breath and eased it out. Some of the tension gripping his chest and holding his lungs captive loosened. "My boss wants me to do something I'm pretty sure is illegal, and if it isn't, it's ethically wrong. But he won't reconsider. I told him I wouldn't do it, but he's threatening some pretty dire consequences if I don't."

The pastor didn't flinch. The expression of intense attention on his face didn't shift to disdain, disgust or even superiority. He looked concerned. For Toby.

"How do his demands make you feel?"

"Disgusted. Afraid I'll lose my job. Shocked. And worried that some people in my life won't understand the situation and think the worst about me."

"Gina."

"Gina."

Jeremy held up his hand, palm outward. "I'm not going to press you to elaborate on the who, the what, and I don't think even you know the why. Will this act cause physical harm to anyone?"

Toby snorted in disgust. "Me, if I get caught."

"Beat up? Shot? Arrested? Killed?"

"Uh, any or all of the above." He rolled his shoulders. "I don't know what this person would do to me. They would probably have someone else do it on their behalf, but the result to me would be the same."

"Okay. If you don't do it, you face complete career ruination."

"Yes. It's the only reason I'm trying to figure out what to do besides just standing my ground on the outright refusal I gave him this morning."

"It raises you in my eyes to hear you say that."

Toby leaned forward. "Look, Pastor Walker, I know all of you think I hang around with Gina for no other reason than I'm hoping I'll hear some juicy pieces of news. That's a little true, but Gina knows. She razzes me about it all the time. I like her. I think of her as a true friend. But I'm not looking for a serious relationship. I have a five-year plan I'm working on, and dating with the intention of something more permanent isn't part of my plan right now. Gina says it isn't in hers either. But sometimes I worry about how much time I spend with her."

"You worry—about Gina?"

"Well, yeah. She says she's too busy to find the man God has picked out for her. And she's positive it isn't me. So it's fine to bring me along when you all have a big gathering where she'd be the only one without a date. I get to talk to you guys and keep an eye out for stories. I mean, the Delaneys are a local political power. Add Judge Pierce and Edward Delaney, and your wife and her parents, and all of you *are* the news in this town. Don't you want someone you know and are comfortable with to be the one asking you questions?"

Jeremy's gaze was as sharp as steel. "Actually, I don't ever want to have to answer a lot of questions."

"I get that—sort of. But if a story is going to be written, wouldn't you rather it was me, whose internal editor is Gina? You know I'm not about to write anything that paints any of her friends in a bad light. She'd skewer me."

"I'll buy it, when you put it that way. But what does any of this have to do with your problem?"

Toby dropped his gaze to the floor, then back up, resting his forearms on his thighs. "Not much. I still have to decide what to do and how to handle it. But it helps me to know I'm not alone. When I left the paper after my meeting with Ivan, I was shell-shocked. I didn't know what to do or where to turn. Thank you for the hope you've given me by being here and just listening. There was nowhere else I could turn."

"God's like that. He'll let you go as far down the wrong road as you need to go. But once you realize you're off course, He'll make sure there's a map or a GPS device right there at your fingertips. He cares for you just like He does everyone else on the earth."

Toby offered his hand. He had a new respect and a little bit of awe at the depth of wisdom the pastor expressed while letting him talk out his problem. Maybe his dad wasn't right about the church thing. And if he was wrong about that, was he wrong about anything else? But those were questions for later.

He'd thank God for leading him here today. To Pastor Walker.

It was nice having God in his corner for a change.

* * *

Gina let herself in the front door of her parents' house. The crisp fragrance of lemon furniture polish welcomed her, evoking thoughts of sugared fruit candies and spiced wassail on cold nights.

Her mother was in the laundry room folding towels. "Hey. What are you doing here at this time of day?"

"I'm playing hooky, but don't tell my bosses."

"Like they'd do anything to you. You have them wrapped around your finger just like you do the rest of us."

"Momma, that isn't nice to say. It's true, but still, you shouldn't confirm my suspicions. It will only make me worse. Just ask Toby."

"I would, but you never bring him around. I had to learn about him from your sister."

"He's just a friend. There isn't anything to tell. We spend more time fighting than talking. When I get married, I want to literally settle down. No bickering or squabbling. Just blissful cohabitation."

Her mother laughed. "Oh, honey. You're thinking of a fairy tale if you believe there's a successful marriage on earth that doesn't include a few rounds of bickering and growling at each other."

"Well, that's what I'm holding out for. Besides, God has the man for me all picked out. I just have to wait for Him to drop him in my lap."

"That's another of your fantasies. But who am I to try and change your mind? Now, tell me what you're really doing here in the middle of a workday."

"You've met Mr. Tobias, haven't you?"

"Momma's friend?"

"That's him. I read to the two of them when I visit her. Anyway, Gigi's invited him to spend Christmas with us. He has a grandson who is close enough to visit him a lot, but I've never met him. Mr. Tobias talks about him all the time. I don't know if he has any other family, though." She smoothed her hand across the soft towel resting on the top of the stack on the dryer. "Gigi asked me if I thought you or Daddy would be upset if she brought him as her guest. I told her it would be fine. It will be, won't it?"

Her mother hugged her tight. "Of course it's fine. I'm so glad she has a special friend to keep her company. She took losing Daddy really hard. You know we wanted her to come live here, but she insisted on going to the retirement villas. She said she'd get bored here and have to come out of retirement. This just confirms that she has settled in well at Sunny Days."

"The three of us usually go for walks around the lake on the warmer afternoons. Saturday we sat in the solarium because it was raining. Gigi was worried about how y'all would feel about having her friend stay over. I told her we'd have two guest rooms ready for them."

"Then it's settled. I'll change the sheets on the beds and run the comforters through the dryer with some freshening sheets. Everything will be ready for their arrival." Her mother lifted the clothes basket full of folded towels and rested it against her hip. "Now, what about your young man. Are you inviting him to dinner?"

"Momma, we're just friends. And his parents live here, or nearby. Besides, Toby's fine for public gatherings, but this is for family. If I introduced him to the clan Lawson he'd bump up the schedule on his five-year plan to get out of Pemberly."

"Well, no one is hauling you off away from your family."

"I'm not going anywhere. That's why he's the perfect date for all my Abby and Katherine gatherings. No strings for either of us." Gina laughed. "We barely like each other."

Chapter 4

"You're late." The gravely accusation stopped Toby in the doorway. He bumped the door closed with his foot before shooting his grandfather a grin.

"Worried I wouldn't bring your contraband?"

Pops waved him off, marking his page in the hard-back murder mystery Toby had brought him last week. He set the book and the magnifying sheet he used to make the words of the large print edition larger on the end table at his side. "Scamp. Back in my day, when a man said he was going to be somewhere, he was there ten minutes early."

Toby came forward and took the seat opposite Pops. "And you walked to school uphill both ways—in the snow."

"Watch it, boy. You're close enough I can reach you with this cane." His threat was made hollow by the slow smile Toby had inherited. His sky blue eyes twinkled.

Setting the plastic grocery bag he had brought with him on the floor, Toby pulled out two individual pints of whole milk and a package of chocolate sandwich cookies. Those he set on the ottoman between them.

"What, not the kind with twice the filling?"

"Pops, it's bad enough I'm slipping you pure sugar and shortening along with cholesterol-loaded milk. Eat your cookies. And I'm not leaving the whole pack. The nurse questioned me about the cookie crumbs she found on your shirt last week."

Pops grabbed the edges of the armrests, ready to hoist himself to his feet.

"Whoa, old man. Where are you going?" Toby was up and crowding him enough he couldn't stand.

"I was getting us some napkins so you can take the evidence with you."

"Just chill, I'll get the napkins." He went into the small kitchen eating area and opened one cabinet door after another until he found them. He brought two small coffee cups back with him, too, offering one to his grandfather.

Pops set the cup on the table and unfolded his paper napkin into a large square, then tucked it into the neck of his shirt like a bib. He poured milk into the cup, and then dunked his cookie, keeping it submerged for a seven-count. He popped the softened circle into his mouth and closed his eyes in delight.

Toby did the same, the flavors of too-sweet filling and chocolate mixed with the chill of the milk taking him back to summers spent with Pops and Grams. Ivan's demands and the reality of being pushed to cross a line he'd never believed he'd even come near tried to steal the warmth of this moment with his grandfather. He closed his eyes, not to savor the taste but to keep the ugliness of the present out of his mind and away from the happy memories of times with this great man.

"You okay?" His grandfather dunked another cookie.

Toby wiped his mouth before plucking one out of the bag and twisting it apart to lick the middle. Stalling. "Everything's good."

His grandfather set his cup of milk on the table. Leaning forward, he caught Toby's wrist in a firm grip. "No, it's not. Your shoulders are drooping so low, you look like you're bearing the weight of the world."

He cocked the corner of his mouth up in an attempt to convince Pops he was off by a mile instead of dead center. Time to move the conversation away from him and back to why he'd dropped in on a Monday afternoon. "Dad called me Saturday."

"Hmm." His shoulders rose and fell in a slight shrug.

"So then you know why he called?"

"Of course I know. I'm old, not senile."

"Look, Pops, I know our family isn't as close as some—"

"Most." He cut him off, his brows angled down in a sharp V.

"Okay, most other families. But who's this 'lady friend' of yours? Why do you want to spend Christmas with her instead of us? Instead of me?"

Pops leveled an ice-blue gaze on him. "Did your father invite someone he wants to impress to Christmas dinner? It's the only reason it would matter to him and Ruth if I'm there or not."

"Pops! How can you say that?"

"Are you telling me it isn't true?"

Toby didn't know. It wasn't out of the realm of possibility if his father was vying for a promotion and trying to show himself as being part of a normal family. And that would definitely include having his father present. Never mind if they were happy together or not. Things just had to look picture-perfect.

"See, even you aren't sure."

"The holidays are a time to be with family. Maybe deep down you hurt his feelings by wanting to be somewhere else. And now I have to listen to Dad yammer on about my career alone."

"Harrumph. Jeffrey and Ruth have never been as happy as the afternoon they toted the last box of my belongings into this apartment. They have the house and no one to remind them of the way your grandmother liked things done in *her* house. And it sounds like even you won't miss me for myself. You're just bothered that there won't be anyone to side with you when your father starts talking about how much better you could be doing at your job."

Nice try, Pops. But his words betrayed him. Toby sat down and reached for his grandfather's hands. "Is that really why you're going somewhere else for Christmas? You miss Grams. I miss her, too. And so do Mom and Dad. If it brings back painful memories being there, we can have dinner at my apartment or here."

"I miss your grandmother every day. Christmas won't be any different, except this year I want to spend it where more than one person is happy to see me. You could come with me."

Oh, if Pops knew how tempting that offer was. The only thing that made a dinner spent with his parents bearable was that he and Pops would be sitting across from each other, trading subtle looks and eye rolls depending on the extent of his father's pontificating about his high-powered job that wasn't. His VP position was barely a step up from middle management, but he believed the company would fold without his daily presence.

It was strange knowing how basic his grandfather was in his beliefs and the "same as every other man" way he saw himself, when his father was the polar opposite. His dad viewed himself as a real-life Tony Stark, minus the money. It was going to be a long holiday dinner. But Pops had more than earned the right to go where he wanted to go. Toby just wished he could go with him.

"Eat up. I have to get going."

"Got a big date?" His grandfather's eyes regained some of their mischievous sparkle.

"I wish. I drew the short straw for the movie-review column this week. They're showing an advanced screening of some sappy chick flick tonight. I thought I'd get it out of the way so my weekend's free."

"Well, if you're going to be free Saturday, you could stop by here about noon. Genevieve's granddaughter should be here. She's just what you need."

Oh, no. No, no, no. He was not having Pops set him up with the granddaughter of his lady friend. If she didn't have anything better to do with her Saturday afternoons than hang out with a bunch of octogenarians, reading the Bible, playing Scrabble or checkers, she was not for him. No way, no how.

"That's a nice offer, but I'll have to pass."

His grandfather rose and followed him to the door. Toby's feet carried him a little faster than they would have if Pops hadn't been in setup mode. What was it with old people anyway? Didn't they understand there was an order to these things, especially if you wanted your future to work out the way you intended? Draw up a detailed plan and check off tasks as you achieved them. A serious relationship or anything romantic was after the last page of his five-year plan. And he was sticking with the plan.

At their usual after-movie coffeehouse, Toby held Gina's chair, then helped her scoot forward. He was such a contradiction. Lazily defiant and antirelationship, yet he displayed the innate manners of a true gentleman without prompting. Which was frustrating because she'd like nothing better than to take all Toby's gentlemanly qualities and mush them together inside a man with relationship potential. One who shaved more than twice a week. Scruffy was cute— on a stray you picked up at the pound.

She tilted her head back until her gaze met his. "Thank you, but your weak attempt at chivalry now and the popcorn and soda at the movie won't get you off the hook. You should have let me know you were running late. I stood outside, shivering in the cold, waiting for you."

But she wasn't done. After he came around the

small table and lowered himself into the seat facing her, she continued. "And where were you anyway?"

He shot her a cocky grin. His dimple was camouflaged by several days' stubble. "I was bribing an old man's affections with milk and cookies."

Gigi and Mr. Tobias popped into her mind, reminding her of how careful she was about the sugar content in the foods she brought them because of their diabetes. "This man isn't a diabetic, is he?"

Toby angled his head to the side. "Only slightly. He controls it with medication."

"It takes medication to keep it under control?" She smacked her hand down on the table. "You are so clueless sometimes. If he needs medication to control his diabetes, he has to be very careful how much sugar he eats. And some cookies have a lot of sugar."

He reached across the table and laid his hand on her arm just above the wrist. "Calm down there, Nurse Ratched, before you accuse me of trying to poison Pops. I asked his doctor if it was okay and he was fine with it."

"But if he's—"

"Pops would be the first to remind you he's old, not dead. A few cookies and milk once a week isn't going to send him to an early grave."

She sat back as the waiter arrived with their mugs of coffee and two slices of Oreo Cookie Cheesecake. Toby's lips twisted into a smirk and one eyebrow arched in a supercilious, annoying way.

"Oh, shut up and eat your cheesecake."

"I can see the romance of the movie had no effect on you." He forked a bite into his mouth and chased it down with some coffee.

"I enjoyed the on-screen romance just fine. It's the sections of dialogue I missed thanks to the loud snores coming from the seat beside me that have me undecided. I'll have to go see it again, alone, to know what they said to each other."

"I was not snoring."

"You were asleep and snoring—louder than a lumberjack's chain saw—before they finished the opening scene."

"Is that why you kept elbowing me in the ribs?"

She rested the warmth of her cup against her lower lip and met his questioning gaze. "I didn't want you to miss the big moments in the movie. Otherwise, how could you write a fair review? And I know how much you enjoy capturing the nuances of love in your stories."

He choked on the coffee he was in the middle of swallowing. She laughed. Oh, it was so nice to see him all choked up, no matter how it happened.

Toby wiped dribbles of coffee from his mouth and chin with a napkin. "Nice timing, Curly. Warn a guy the next time you plan to talk out of your head."

"You're the one always claiming you write the truth. That was a romance we just watched on the big screen. I expect your review to reflect how well the actors did or didn't convey the depth of emotions that led to their happy ending."

He snorted. "Oh, please. It's a romantic comedy. The only similarities to real life being the woman saying she wanted one thing when she really wanted something else. And when she said she didn't want something when she really did. The comedy was how stupid the man looked falling all over himself to please her."

She patted his arm. "Poor Toby. Guys never think *they* act that way. But most of you do."

"No, we don't. A guy does not go charging after a woman who has told him to take a hike. He shakes it off and moves on. That's what real men do."

She threw her head back and laughed, then faced him, giving him a hard stare. "For the right woman a man would do anything."

"Not. Or at least, not me. I saw what losing Grams did to Pops. I'm not opening myself up to that. And besides, that kind of devotion is rare. And the plans I have for my career don't allow time for me to go all loony tunes over a woman. Not that I ever would."

He'd made comments here and there about his childhood. Gina blamed his parents' distant marriage for warping his view on relationships. She almost pitied him for not having a loving home and family. She was truly blessed. But Toby was an adult. He was around other couples, was exposed to countless examples of true love and real commitment. She was convinced that his constant use of his parents' unhappy marriage as his benchmark was a defense to keep himself out of any type of relationship where he'd have to dig deep and give something of himself. She shook her head. Why should she care if he expected, or wanted, the shallow, emotionless existence his inane five-year plan guaranteed? Not her problem.

"Your personal views on relationships have stunted your emotional development. That's why you always beg me to come with you to the chick flicks. You need me to decipher the emotional subtext of the movie so you can fool your readers into thinking you understand women and know something about relationships. Which you don't."

Toby wadded up his napkin and tossed it beside the fork on his empty plate. He slid it out of the way and pulled his coffee closer. "I understand women and their emotions just fine. I'm not the one spending my Saturday nights at home. I'm out with someone every weekend."

"I take it back. You're doing a fine job of exhibiting sensitivity right now."

He leaned in. "If you don't want to get burned, stay out of the kitchen."

She twitched her finger in front of his face. "Poor Toby, you're so confused you're mixing your metaphors."

His eyes narrowed behind the curtain of his too-long bangs. "Not me. The man did what he had to so the woman would be happy and they could move on. That was the concept of the movie we just watched."

"*I* watched. *You* slept."

"I was awake when he swallowed his pride and dropped to one knee. That's all you women care about."

"What?"

"Watching the guy cave."

"Are you out of your little pea-brained head? Yes, we want a proposal. You saw Jeremy's. How you wrangled his permission to run a photo of him on the front page of the *Sentinel* is beyond me. But he wasn't looking too put-upon in that picture. In fact, that was the biggest smile I've ever seen on his face."

"Yeah, well, love can make a man go stupid."

Her blood pounded harder and faster in her temples

the longer he talked. She was going to start thanking God every night that Toby Hendricks was not the man for her. And as irritating as he was, she knew him better than he realized. He'd picked a fight about love and feelings so she'd stop questioning him. Well, that was not going to work.

"What has you so edgy tonight? And don't go trotting down the Men and Women Come from Different Emotional Planets Highway. Is Ivan pushing you to plant a bug in my purse, hoping you'll get some really good dirt on my political friends?"

He swallowed hard. His eyes darted away from hers. If he even tried something half that sneaky, she would hang him over the park bridge by his shoelaces and leave him there until spring.

He cleared his throat, went for a drink of coffee out of his empty cup. "No, Ivan knows I would never do anything like that."

It was her turn to arch an eyebrow in question. "Does he?"

Gina's words sent a chill all the way to Toby's bones. Where was the waiter? He needed some scalding hot coffee now. She was razzing him. She had to be. There was no way she knew what Ivan wanted from him, how much more he wanted Toby to use her. And he vowed she never would.

He reclined back in his chair and cupped the back of his head in his hands before giving her his laziest grin. "Gina, babe." Oh, how she bristled whenever he called her that. "I think you're trying to focus on my shortcomings to compensate for your lack of dating activity. I mean, how credible a source on dating and women's emotions can you be if the only time I hear of you going out is when you tag along with me on movie-review night?"

He reached down and rubbed his shin. Okay, that may have been too much. Her feet were as fast and lethal as those fingers of hers.

She leaned forward, the cinnamon in her eyes tinting toward cayenne. "I can't wait for the day you fall so deep into love, there isn't a rope long enough to pull you out. And I'm going to be there with a camera. The *Sentinel* will use the photo with a headline that reads, 'Reporter Lands in Love: It's All Over but the Crying.'"

"Not gonna happen."

"You're on, Hendricks." She held out her hand.

He looked from her extended hand back to her face. "What?"

"You're going to write your review, citing our differing opinions, and we'll let your readers decide how love really works."

"Uh, no. Even though I'd take you by a landslide. Most of my readership is male." He leaned back again. "I won't be getting all touchy-feely in any article with my name on it."

She pressed her lips together and cocked them to the side. He'd never noticed how full the lower one was. Must be the deep red lipstick that hadn't lost its shine through a slice of cheesecake and a cup of coffee. He shook his head, trying to regain his focus. *Fight with Gina. Win.*

"One post on my Facebook page and I'd have your in-box swamped with readers outraged by your stereotypical Dark Ages ideals on women and relation-ships."

"Well, as much as I'd love to prove you wrong in the pages of the paper, my stories cover real news."

The eye roll was exaggerated. Just like all her other expressions of disgust at his opinions were. "So you're chickening out?"

"No, I'm sparing you a very public humiliation."

"Whatever. A man in love would do anything for the woman he loves. He would tell her how he feels, even if it made him uncomfortable."

"And you're nuts. Guys don't get all sappy and talk about their feelings. Most of us don't even admit to having any. All you women want to do is project your mushy, fluttery heart palpitations on us simple, de-pendable guys. I'm not playing along."

"Fine. Besides I don't know if I can personally buy into the happily-ever-after in this movie." She scrunched her nose up as if she'd caught a whiff of something nasty.

"Do tell."

"I have a hard time with dishonesty. He cheated, he lied and then he begged her to forgive him, claim-ing he knew it was wrong." She waved her hand in a dismissive gesture. "If he knew it was wrong, why'd he do it? Was it worth the risk?"

"He made a mistake."

"A big one." She pointed her finger at him before he could say anything. "Which led him to make an-other bad choice. Don't you see the pattern? As hard as it is to resist temptation, it's harder to fix the mis-takes giving in to it can create. Some of them can't be fixed. They stay broken forever."

Sucker punch to the stomach. Her words knocked the wind out of him. His lungs were screaming for air. If he'd wondered how she'd react if he did what Ivan wanted, now he knew. There would be no forgiveness. Not from Gina.

Suddenly he was too tired to fight with her. To consider his options where Ivan was concerned. He wanted to go home to his small apartment and be alone. To try to figure out what he was going to do about tomorrow. Go in to work knowing he wouldn't steal the notebook from the senator and not tell Ivan? Or start looking for another job. It wasn't time yet. He still had goals in his plan he needed to achieve. It would be great if God would give him a sign or something.

"Oh, I almost forgot. If you haven't already lined up a date for New Year's Eve, they're having a party at the senator's house. It's his sixtieth birthday, too, so Abby and her mom are throwing him a huge bash. Frannie's doing the food."

He blinked to bring her back into focus. Was it a sign or a test? Either way, it bought him a little time with Ivan. He smiled for real this time. *Thank you, God.*

Chapter 5

Gina shifted the armload of files to her right hip and tapped on the half-open door of Katherine Delaney's office. "Hey, Kat, I have a few questions…"

The words slid to a halt in the middle of the room along with her footsteps. Katherine was curled up on the small sofa, the plastic garbage can nearby. She raised her head, then let it fall back onto the cushion with a pathetic moan.

Gina dropped the folders on the corner of her desk and rushed over to her. "What's wrong? Is it the flu? Do you need me to fix you some of Gigi's tea?"

Kat's response was a whimper. Otherwise, she lay perfectly still. Gina touched her forehead. Clammy but cool. She moved the container further away from Katherine. No way was its close proximity helping matters.

"Do you want me to call Nick?" She brushed the

hair stuck to the side of Kat's face away, tucking it behind her ear. "Let me get a cool washcloth for your face. I can call my doctor and see if they can work you in."

"Uh-huh." She looked and sounded miserable.

"Kat, you have to tell me what's wrong so I can help you. Think of how upset Nick would be, knowing you were sick and I didn't call him."

"His fault," Katherine grumbled.

"You know kissing a sick person might make them feel a little better immediately. But it usually makes you feel worse in about a week."

Katherine moved her head in what could have been a shaking motion, but then stopped and squeezed her eyes closed.

"Let me make you some peppermint tea. It's the best thing for nausea."

It said a lot about how bad Katherine felt that she didn't protest. As green as she looked, she probably didn't have the strength. As the cup of water heated in the microwave, Gina tapped her finger against Nick's image on her phone. He answered on the second ring.

"Hey, Gina. Calling to congratulate me?"

"Congrat—"

"Isn't it awesome? I'm going to be a father. Kat is a little nervous about the whole thing, but she's going to be a great mother."

Katherine and Nick were expecting a baby. The realization weakened her enough she leaned against the counter for support, nodding at the phone. "A baby."

The microwave beeped and the soft mewling moan of her friend reached her from just down the hall. Oh, poor Katherine. Nick was babbling like a toddler with a new toy while Katherine was probably hoping for death or at least unconsciousness until the morning sickness phase was over.

"That's great, Nick. I'm so happy for you. Listen, on your way home today, can you pick up some saltine crackers, you know, without any flavors besides salt? And you need some cheese slices and a box of peppermint tea. Oh, and some ginger ale."

He paused in his excitement. "She's really sick, isn't she?" He didn't wait for a reply. "I knew it. That's why she rushed me out of the house this morning. I'm coming over there and taking her home. She needs to be in bed."

"Nick, stop. Yes, she's very nauseated. But she'd be even more miserable at home, stuck in bed. I'm making her some tea now. Just be supportive and maybe have the tea waiting for her when she gets up in the mornings. My sister-in-law, Elise, had morning sickness for three months. Keep Kat hydrated and time will help her get past this stage. Okay?"

"Okay. Thanks, Gina, for looking out for her. You know she loves you like a sister."

"I know. It goes both ways. Now, don't forget your shopping list."

She stirred sugar and a single drop of cream into the aromatic brew and asked God to help Kat's nausea go away. She set the cup of tea and three stale saltine crackers on a small tray before heading down the hall, toward the sounds of misery coming from her boss's office.

"Okay, this is plain, old-fashioned peppermint tea. I want you to sip it slowly." Gina sat down on the cushion beside Katherine's head and swabbed her face with the cool cloth she'd brought with her. Then she took hold of Katherine's shoulders and helped ease her upright into a sitting position a little at a time, stopping whenever Katherine moaned.

"Try to sip this while I go get rid of—" She motioned her hand toward the garbage can. "I'll be back in a few minutes. Go slow with the tea. And if the nausea isn't so bad after a few sips, then try to nibble on one of those crackers, but stop if you feel queasy at all. Okay?"

Katherine didn't nod but reached for the cup with unsteady hands. "When I told him this morning, he started whooping and yelling. I have no idea what the neighbors thought, but I had to close my eyes, he was making me dizzy. And the nausea..."

"Don't try to talk. Just sip the tea and breathe through your nose. Let the scent and taste of peppermint settle your stomach."

With the garbage can cleaned and sterilized within an inch of its existence, Gina brought it back into Katherine's office. She was sitting in her chair at her desk, reading one of the files Gina had dropped there in her haste to make sure she was okay.

"Well, you're not as green as you were before. That's a good sign. How do you feel?" She dropped into the seat facing Kat.

"Definitely better. Thank you. It's so strange. Ten minutes ago, I thought I was going to die. And now, I'm much better. I still feel a little woozy, but the tea really helped. Thank you."

"No problem. It's the only thing Elise could tolerate in the mornings during her first trimester. I called Nick and gave him a shopping list."

Katherine's head shot up and her wide eyes met Gina's gaze. She touched her hand to the side of her head. "Oh. No more quick head movements." She drew a breath in through her nose and eased it out between her teeth. "I did one of those early tests over the weekend. I was going to tell you this morning."

Gina came around the desk and wrapped her arms around her, careful not to jostle her too much. "I'm not worried about that. Nick just caught me by surprise. I was prepared to rattle off a list of foods for helping you survive the flu when he started whooping and hollering in my ear. I'm so happy for you. You're getting a family that's all your own. No one deserves that more."

She handed Katherine a tissue. "How do you automatically know what I need right now?" Katherine dabbed at her eyes.

"Elise, Gary's wife. She was sick as a dog for three months. Then the first morning of the fourth month, she woke up with a craving for a deep-dish, double-pepperoni pizza."

Katherine blanched and reached for her cup of tea.

"Sorry. I just wanted you to know you won't always feel that bad. And I think knowing it will get better helps you get through the miserable time."

After a few slow breaths in and out, Katherine moved the file folder out of the way. Gina was back in her seat, facing her. "The past year and a half has been the biggest emotional roller coaster I could imagine. So many things have changed for me, for Nick, Abby and Jeremy, too. You've been our constant."

"Yeah, that's me. I'm the best in a pinch."

Katherine reached out and grabbed Gina's hand

with a question in her eyes. "Gina, do you feel like we've taken advantage of you?" Her brow wrinkled and she worried her lower lip.

She gave Katherine what she hoped the woman would read as an "are you crazy" look. "No, Katherine. None of you have ever made me feel like that. We're friends. In fact, my circle of friends has grown exponentially during this last year and a half. Toby can't dream up enough outings to get himself invited to in the hopes of catching a juicy piece of news for one of his articles."

Katherine watched her, which made Gina want to fill the silence with something. She just didn't know what. Being blindsided with the news that her boss, her best friend, was racking up yet another blessing of home and family was a shocker first thing in the morning. And her discussion, okay, argument with Toby last night had left her unsettled. Did he really think she didn't have any romantic prospects? What did it say about her that Mr. No-Commitment saw her as less likely to find herself in a relationship than he?

"What's wrong?" Katherine's question drew her out of her thoughts.

"Nothing." She offered a wide smile. "I'm just plotting how I'm going to spoil this little Harper-Delaney delight."

Katherine took another sip of tea before setting the cup down and moving it away. "Do you care for Toby?"

Whack. "What?"

"I know you snarl and snap like two badgers fighting over a meal, but is that just for show? Deep down he is nice, and I don't think all his visits are driven by a possible scoop on Pemberly politics. He gets very snarky when you talk about Shaun Fowler. I'd pick someone else for you, but if you like him and he likes you, it's your relationship. I would respect your choice. But I will caution you, he doesn't act committed to anything but his next story. Make sure he isn't playing games with you."

Gina nodded. What else could she do? She'd lain awake for a long time last night, thinking about these very things. When they'd been in the movie theater, with all those couples snuggled up to each other, she'd been comfortable—even with Toby asleep. The snuffly sounds of his sleeping were familiar from all the other chick flicks she'd watched with him for his assignments. And what did it say about her that she actually looked forward to the intense arguments that always followed the happily-ever-afters on the screen?

She'd shaken him awake after the ending credits rolled. He'd slowly opened his eyes. For the first time, she noticed just how clear a blue they were. In fact, if they were on another man, they'd be attractive. On Toby, they were wasted, hidden behind a hank of shaggy bangs that would do a sheepdog proud. Why on earth didn't he cut his hair? She was convinced that under all the shagginess was a good-looking guy.

She shook her head and looked at Katherine. "No, Toby's fine for a movie date or to keep the numbers even at one of y'all's or Jeremy and Abby's gatherings. He has a vested interest in being there and I don't feel obligated to stay by his side the whole night. It's a symbiotic relationship. You know I don't like being the only one without a date."

Katherine gave her a stern look, which was impressive since she hadn't lost quite all the green tinge to her complexion from this morning's bout of nausea. "I just want to make sure you're the shark and he's the suckerfish and not the other way around."

"Toby and I have an understanding."

"An understanding?" Katherine did not look pleased by her choice of words.

"He's allowed to hang out with potential story leads when he escorts me. But if I read anything in one of his articles that I believe he got from snooping while with me, no one will ever see or hear from him again."

Katherine laughed. Then clapped her hand over her mouth. "Go away. If you make me laugh, I'll get sick again. And I'm trying very hard to avoid that."

Gina stood up and scooped the files she'd left on the desk earlier into her arms. "Do you want me to call Judge Pierce's clerk and reschedule your court times to the afternoon for the next couple of weeks?"

She looked as if she was going to argue, or offer an assurance that today was a fluke and she'd be fine the rest of the week. But Gina dropped her gaze to the sterilized garbage can beside Katherine's desk.

"Yes, please. But don't tell him why. I have a doctor's appointment Friday. I want an official confirmation and some sort of timeline before we announce it to everyone. If you think Uncle Charles is bad, Edward is going to be impossible."

"Nick's dad? I thought you two were getting along well."

"We are. That's the thing. This will be his first grandchild. Nick and I will be lucky if he doesn't contact his college and start the admission process the next day."

Gina smiled. She had lots of family and couldn't imagine her life without all the joys and excitement of enlarging that family. Both Katherine and Nick came from small families. A new addition was extra special. "No problem. If Jon, his clerk, presses me for a reason, I'll explain that you're adjusting your schedule for some additional appointments."

At Katherine's arched brow, Gina shrugged. "It'll work for the short term and it's true if you have a doctor's appointment. Besides, you need to come in later in the mornings to give yourself time to feel better. I can always call you if a crisis pops up. I come from a big family. I know all the tricks."

Gina winked as she closed the door on her way out. She flopped down at her desk and wondered how long it would be before Jeremy was making midnight food-craving runs for Abby. Everything was coming up baby. For everyone but her.

"Well, Hendricks, I see you made the right choice." Ivan leaned a thick-fingered hand on the top of Toby's cubicle divider.

"Yeah, Ivan. Turns out I have rent to pay, so I need my job."

Ivan glanced around the mostly empty office, then leaned down into the square that was Toby's space. "I heard the senator's having a big New Year's Eve bash at that fancy house of his. It won't be much of a stretch to sweet-talk your little girlfriend into letting you tag along. Get in. Get out. Piece of cake."

"Piece of cake? You aren't the one who's risking

his neck here. You really need to rethink your plan. I could do an interview, mention I've seen the note-book—"

Ivan slashed his hand through the air. "No. I don't want him to know I know about the notebook until the secrets he's been hoarding away in there over the years are laid bare for all of Pemberly to see."

Toby shook his head. "Anytime the evil villain thinks he has the perfect plan to foil Superman, it backfires. This isn't going to work. Senator Black-mon isn't a power-hungry politician. He's a good man. He cares about all of his constituents, especially the ones in this town."

Sucking in a deep breath and straightening his spine, Ivan squinted a cold glare at him. "I'm not Lex Luthor and you aren't Clark Kent. So get the su-perhero-saving-the-day idea out of your head. That notebook is news. Big news. And I want the truth re-vealed on my watch."

Toby kept pushing. "What did he do to you?"

"That's not your—"

"Yes, it is, Ivan. You're forcing me to risk my neck, my reputation, on some vendetta you have against Blackmon. I deserve to know why."

"Get me the book and maybe I'll tell you." Ivan grinned enough to show the glint off his gold tooth, then headed toward his office.

Toby sat, staring at his computer screen. This wasn't right. And he had known it wasn't the minute Ivan laid out his plan. Before he'd talked to the pas-tor. Before Gina had said she didn't think she could forgive dishonesty.

He could leave. Run. But running was for cowards

or quitters. There had to be a way out of this without him doing something wrong. Without him disappointing the people who mattered to him.

He couldn't leave Pemberly, not yet anyway. He only saw Pops twice a week now. If he moved, it would be even less. He was the only one Toby considered real family. The only one who really cared about him.

He grabbed his jacket off the back of his chair. He'd see Pops three times this week. It would be an early Christmas present—for him. Pops would just want to know where his cookies were. And maybe he should call the doctor again to make sure it was still okay for Pops to have that burst of sugar each week. They made sugar-free sandwich cookies, didn't they? Pops would be as willing to try one as Toby was to admit the ugly truth. Gina was right. But only about the extra sugar in the cookies.

He drove out of the parking garage and into the late-morning sunlight. Taking a left at the next light, he drove away from downtown with the steeple of Grace Community Church in his rearview mirror. Now that he was seeking God's guidance, Toby began to see the church as more than just a building in the middle of town. It was a solid fixture, a presence, in the people's lives around here.

There were other churches, some as big as or bigger than Grace Community was. But Gina, her family, the Blackmons, the Delaneys and the Walkers all attended Grace Community. A place where families came together into a bigger family. A networking system built on love and concern, not career advancement and superiority. He got that. He didn't always agree with it, but he got the mini-sermons Gina peppered him with whenever she could work one into their conversations.

He grinned. He liked her. She was a really good friend. She worried about him. The only other person who had ever worried about him was Pops.

Pulling into the parking lot of Sunny Days Retirement Villas, Toby tried to banish his spiritual musings. He wasn't a soul searcher. He was a reporter willing to do anything to get the story. That thought stopped him before his feet touched the pavement.

Gina's claims were wrong. He wouldn't do *anything* for a story. Because he wasn't going to steal the notebook from Senator Blackmon. But not totally because it was wrong. It shamed him to admit the truth, even to himself. He couldn't steal it because he was afraid of getting caught.

He nodded to the receptionist at the front desk as he strode past. This late in the morning, Pops was either finishing a daily session of chair aerobics or in the middle of a heated checkers tournament with his main squeeze, who was also his biggest competition. The loser bought the winner a cappuccino in the coffee shop afterward.

Sunny Days was laid out like a small self-contained resort town. Situated around Lake Sun, there was a grocer, an ice cream shop, a coffeehouse, several restaurants, a beauty salon, even a general practitioner who gave the residents priority appointments and made house calls.

The retirement village where Pops leased a two-bedroom apartment was located on this side of the lake. The acreage included a buffet-style cafeteria on the ground floor of the apartment building. They served three gourmet meals a day in balance with the number of reservations at the small restaurants. The ground floor also boasted a solarium overlooking an English garden that sloped down to the walking, biking and dog paths around the lake. There was an indoor pool attached to an impressive gym and rehabilitation center. And a chapel at the opposite end of the building rounded out the amenities available on campus. It really wasn't a terrible place to visit. In fact, it was a little like a resort.

The majority of older seniors in Pemberly and the surrounding areas moved here, usually after losing a spouse. Toby figured they got tired of rattling around in big houses all by themselves, like Pops had.

Toby was glad there had been options like this for Pops after losing Grams and having a stroke. Toby's mom and dad had made it clear they weren't comfortable sharing the house with Pops. Which said quite a bit about his parents since it was Pops' house.

He checked the gym first. There was an older-ladies yoga class in session. He eased out of the room as quietly as he'd entered. The central community area had sofas, upholstered chairs with footstools pushed underneath them and a large flat-screen television for movie night. At the back of the room, he took the three steps down to the lower landing and walked toward the solarium.

Pops was leaned back in a recliner with his head drooped to the side, out cold. Mrs. Montego sat at the end of a small sofa near his chair. Her knitting needles clacked together in a steady rhythm while *The Price Is Right* played on a gigantic television screen.

An oversize checkerboard sat on a small game table between the side of the recliner and the sofa. It was clear red had won and the black pieces were strewn all over their side of the game board. Pops always chose black. A smile tugged at the corner of Toby's mouth as he bent and picked up one of the discarded pieces off the floor.

He kept his voice low so he wouldn't disturb his grandfather's nap. "Did you wear him down during the game until he needed a nap? Or did he pitch such a fit over losing, he had to rest?"

She clamped her fingers over her lips to hold the laughter inside. But mischief twinkled in her eyes. "He's such a sore loser. You aren't like that, are you?"

She patted the cushion next to hers and he sat down on the sofa. "No, ma'am. I cheat when my opponent isn't looking."

"Ooh, my granddaughter would have her hands full keeping you straight. You're just as much of a pistol as Tobias is."

Great. Apparently, Pops and his lady friend were united in their efforts to fix him up with her granddaughter. And he wasn't about to do anything to encourage their efforts.

"I'm sure Pops has told you how busy my job keeps me. I'm not the best candidate for a serious relationship right now. But thank you for thinking of me."

"My goodness, you are the most mannerly young man when worming your way out of something you're desperate to avoid." Her expression shifted from teasing to more serious. The laugh lines faded from her eyes and little creases appeared across her brow. She held her lips together in a straight line.

No wonder Pops wanted to spend Christmas with Mrs. Montego and her family. She was warm and funny, with a comfortable sassiness she had no problem turning on him just as she would Pops.

He'd thought to spend the next week slowly coaxing his grandfather into changing his mind about his Christmas plans. But how selfish was it for him to want Pops to endure a day of strained quiet among family who couldn't even be cordial to one another? Pops had been invited to join a close family who knew how to love and laugh together. What better example of holiday cheer. For that, Toby was jealous.

Chapter 6

A valet opened Gina's door and offered his hand. She slid out of Toby's truck, her satin high heels clicking on the concrete beneath the portico of the senator's home.

Toby waited for the valet to close her door before offering his arm. They hadn't gone ten feet up the walkway when she tugged on his arm and brought their forward momentum to a grinding halt.

"What?"

"I am not walking into this party with your tie looking like a crumpled piece of paper someone tried to smooth out with his hands. What did you do to the thing?

"What's wrong with it?"

She let out a huff of agitation. "This is the tie you wore to the reception, isn't it. You didn't untie it when you got home, did you?" She growled, muttering something about his inability to properly tie a tie. Not that she'd offered to teach him how to do it, but still, she was worse than a mother hen clucking at him as if he was one of her baby chicks. "Hold still while I fix this for you."

He stared at her for a moment before tilting his head back so she'd have better access to the silk noose she was knotting at his neck. "It seems like we've been here before."

"Yes, and you're more wrinkled than you were the last time. I don't understand you. You have nice clothes. But they look like you keep them in a pile on the floor. This is a silk tie. Silk." She waved the wider end in his face. "Silk is a delicate fabric. It deserves better care than just yanking the knot loose and scraping it over your head."

"Are you done with your checklist of my fashion faux pas?"

She cinched the tie tight around his throat. Maybe if she strangled him, it would prevent him from walking inside the senator's house, and he could avoid temptation. He should have begged off. Told her he was sick or something. But no, he didn't plan to steal the notebook. He just wanted to look at it. To see what all the fuss was about. *Curiosity killed the cat.*

For him, it wouldn't be curiosity. His death would come at the hands of a curly-haired imp who relished skewering him for his mistakes. And she would make it slow and painful. Of that, he had no doubt. Maybe if he stuck close to Gina all night, there wouldn't be an opportunity to search for the notebook and he wouldn't get himself murdered by his date.

He offered up a small prayer for help to resist temptation. Funny how spending more time with Gina and talking with Pastor Walker had turned him on to the idea that he didn't have to fight his battles alone. That the weight of all he tried or wanted to do could be shared with a power stronger than he could ever be. But he was new to the idea of blindingly trusting God's control of the situation. He liked having the power to decide for himself. That was why God gave him a brain, wasn't it?

Gina laced her fingers with his and gave a gentle squeeze. Did she sense the turmoil going on inside him? His relentless quest for the truth was what made him so good at his job. Could that be a bad thing?

Jeremy Walker answered the door. "Come on in. It's a bit too cool out there for a woman in a frilly dress." He stepped back, giving them room to enter the foyer.

Toby slid Gina's arms free of her coat before shrugging out of his own leather jacket. The pastor motioned him toward a door right next to the entryway. Toby made a point of waving the hanger at Gina and smirking. She stuck her tongue out at him as he hung both their coats in the large closet. When he turned around, Abby had joined the group and she and Gina were embracing.

After letting go of Gina, she gave him a strong hug. "I'm so glad you could be here tonight, Toby. As much as we see you, it's like you're an unofficial part of the family." Her cheeks flushed pink.

Jeremy draped his arm around her and pulled her close. "What my wife meant to say is how great it is that you and Gina are here to celebrate the senator's birthday and ring in the New Year."

"Yes, that's exactly what I meant to say. Sorry, Toby, we've been going ninety to nothing today, getting everything ready. My brain and my manners are taking a nap."

They laughed, and Abby and Jeremy led them into the dining room where the pocket doors that separated it from a formal sitting area had been hidden within the walls, doubling the size of the room. Buffet tables lined one wall with a carving station positioned at each end.

The Walkers left them with orders to save room for dessert. In a corner was a round table with a towering cake trimmed in red, white and blue. Circling it were small cakes in the shape of sixes and zeros frosted in black and white with silver sprinkles scattered around the base. There was enough cake on that table for half of Pemberly. And judging by the size of the crowd, there wouldn't be much left.

But right now, Toby's focus was on the food. "Frannie is amazing."

His mouth watered at all the selections spread before him. He couldn't choose, so he added a sample of everything to his plate until it was heaped high. "Frannie is amazing."

Gina laughed. "You said that already. But it probably bears repeating." They were approaching the carving station. She added a stuffed mushroom to her plate from the last tray in the buffet, then paused before the chef in a white jacket and hat. "A thin slice of the well done, please."

Toby waved off the chef's offer of a slice of succulent prime rib and nabbed two napkin-wrapped sets of silverware, stuffing them in his pocket. Gina found them a spot at one of many high-top tables positioned throughout the room.

"I'll go get our drinks. What would you like?"

Gina eyed the rich foods covering her red plate. "I think just water. I don't want anything interfering with all these yummy flavors. Frannie outdid herself tonight."

"Definitely. I'll be right back." He popped a crab rangoon into his mouth with a sigh before leaving his plate in Gina's care.

Crystal goblets filled with ice water sat on a small table and Toby claimed two. As he turned, a woman coming past him stumbled and the contents of her glass splattered across his tie and shirt. The chilled liquid drew his eyes down to his chest where red punch was soaking into his tie—his silk tie.

A nearby waiter dipped a white cloth napkin in one of the glasses of water and tried dabbing at his tie. The woman let out a low whimper and began apologizing profusely. Toby took the wet napkin from the waiter and scrubbed at his tie and shirt.

"It's okay. Accidents happen," he assured her while scanning the room for one of the hosts.

City Councilman Nick Delaney was approaching with a determined stride. He maneuvered around small clusters of people, smiling or nodding as appropriate, always the consummate politician.

"I'm guessing the punch did that and not Gina." He motioned his head toward Toby's soaked and stained shirt.

"Yeah, Gina's style is more subtle. She doesn't like to draw attention to her victims."

"I'm not sure there's any hope for the tie or the

shirt at this point, but there's a full-size bath at the end of that hall and around the corner, across from the senator's study." He pointed toward the hallway to the side of the massive staircase. "I'll find Abby and let her know we may need to scrounge up at least a polo shirt if we can't manage anything fancier. And I'll let Gina know you've run into a bit of an accident."

Toby nodded and swallowed hard. Not because he was about to become more of a pariah in this group than his job as a reporter already made him, or the fact that he would be very underdressed once he changed into a dry shirt of doubtful style. No, he swallowed hard against the inevitable dread of facing his biggest temptation after he had prayed and asked God to keep him out of trouble. And instead of being delivered from the risk of messing up, he had just been given directions to the room most likely to hold his greatest temptation. He wasn't sure he had it in him to resist.

"Thanks." He looked down at the stain covering the center of his torso and couldn't get past how the damage to his shirt and tie was a perfect reflection of what the inside of his soul must look like right now.

He left the room and turned down the hallway, keeping his eyes straight ahead. No glancing to see if any doors happened to be slightly ajar. *At the end of that hall and around the corner, across from the senator's study.* The words played like a death knell with each step he took down the hallway.

Inside the bathroom, Toby wrenched the knot on his tie, then tugged it free of his collar. Gina wouldn't have the chance to lecture him about his removal methods again. He tossed it in the trash. After unbuttoning his dress shirt and tugging it out of his waistband, he stripped it off and laid it on the dark granite countertop. His undershirt bore a tinge of pink in the very center, just below the end of his sternum.

A knock at the door was followed by a familiar voice. "Toby, Abby sent you one of her dad's dress shirts. He's about your height, but the shirt might be a little loose in the shoulders."

Toby opened the door to the pastor. "Please tell me she forgot to send a tie."

Jeremy held up a blue paisley already-knotted noose. "Ahem. Gina said something about you having trouble tying them."

He had never thought men could blush, but his face was burning. "Yeah, well, a tie isn't part of my daily uniform."

"I wish I could say the same, but it's a necessary evil on some occasions. I think you could get away with leaving it off if you don't want to wear it."

How was he supposed to explain? And why did it have to be the pastor. Talk about a walking conscience. "Let me see how the shirt fits first, and then I'll decide." He took both pieces of clothing and laid them on the opposite side of the sink from the contaminated one. He traced the design in the tie with his finger, fighting a mental battle over asking for some advice.

Jeremy sensed or somehow understood all was not well with him. He opened the door a little wider and leaned against the door facing. "I've been wondering about something."

Toby kept his head down but raised his eyes to the mirror where he caught the pastor's direct gaze.

"That situation you came to me about earlier in the month. How did it turn out?"

"It's still a work in progress. My deadline to act is four days away."

"Is it?" Jeremy's voice dropped to a deeper, stronger tone.

Toby spun to face him. "Ivan gave me until the fourth before he would act."

"This isn't about Ivan or his actions. It's about what *you've* chosen to do. Either you've refused to do what he wants or you're still trying to find a way to do it without getting caught. I'd like to think it's the first, but I'm worried it's the latter. Toby, your job doesn't make you who you are. Your honor and your integrity do."

"You sound like my grandfather. He reminds me of life lessons like that all the time, too."

The pastor held his gaze for a few thudding beats of Toby's heavy heart before nodding and backing all the way out of the doorway. "Then I'll pray you apply the correct one to this situation." With that, he left him in the tiled room across the hall from the most likely place to find both his job security and his moral downfall.

Toby took off his undershirt and scrubbed out the stain. Then he went after his dress shirt. What was he doing? Talk about futile. After wiping his hands on the towel, he threw his stained dress shirt in the trash, then draped his now stain-free undershirt over the towel rack inside the shower and out of sight.

The clean dress shirt was a close fit. A little loose

in the collar, but only enough to be comfortable, not enough to look as if he was wearing another man's shirt, which he was. The man he had been contemplating stealing from. A man who had invited him into his home for a birthday and holiday celebration with the rest of his closest friends. Toby's chest burned with those thoughts.

He couldn't steal for Ivan. But he did want to find the notebook. Maybe the answer to how to handle Ivan was written in there. Maybe a clue as to why Ivan hated the senator. He closed his eyes and asked God to help him find the book—to find a solution. He tucked the clean shirt into his waistband and straightened the tie and collar.

He stopped in the hallway outside the bathroom. In front of the door to what should be the senator's study. No one was coming down the hall. In fact, the chatter of all the guests was barely a dull hum this far removed from the revelry. He placed his hand on the doorknob and turned it. The catch in his chest when it opened was a mixture of excitement and conscience. *I'm only trying to find out what has Ivan so obsessed so I can get out from under his control. I'm not going to take anything.*

He wasn't sure if he was saying that to himself or God. But he was inside the room and his feet propelled him forward without conscious effort. Maybe his heart knew best. He was doing this to save his job, not to ruin anyone. He wouldn't write anything down. He wouldn't take any pictures. He just wanted to see what all the fuss was about.

With the senator's chair pushed back and the reading lamp on, Toby pulled the center drawer open. There, in the middle of that shallow drawer lay the notebook. He took it, closed the drawer, and sat down on the edge of the chair. He had just opened it to the middle when he heard voices in the hall. Right outside the door he hadn't closed all the way.

Busted. Go directly to jail. Do not pass Go. Do not collect two hundred dollars. Forget Monopoly, he'd be lucky if they allowed him a phone call. He snapped the book closed and reached for the drawer, jostling the pens and other loose items inside with the force of his tug.

The book was still in his hand, hovering over the drawer, when the door swung open and Senator Blackmon and Dekker came inside. And stopped cold.

The deep lines on the senator's furrowed brow convinced Toby he wouldn't have to explain anything. The senator had assessed the situation and decided in the blink of an eye exactly what he was doing. And he wasn't wrong about the actions. Just the motives.

"What do you think you're doing?"

Dekker closed the door, then surged forward, his hand reaching inside his jacket. Toby's stomach hit his shoes. *Please, God, don't let him shoot me.*

"I told you he was trouble. You're too trusting." The icy gravel of Dekker's voice added to the chill running up Toby's spine.

And even though he knew they wouldn't believe him, he tried anyway. "It isn't how it looks." Toby came around the desk, away from Dekker and toward the senator. "Honestly, sir. I wasn't going to take it. I just wanted to see what was inside."

The senator was pacing in a small circuit, clenching and unclenching his fists at his sides. Toby tried to keep his breathing normal, but the longer the senator was silent the worse the possibilities of what would happen next became in Toby's hyperactive imagination.

Dekker caught him by the wrist and twisted it behind his back. He pushed Toby down until the side of his face pressed against the edge of the blotter in the middle of the desk. "You have the right to remain silent."

The senator stopped pacing and whirled toward them. "Dekker, let him up."

"What?" both men asked simultaneously, one with hope, the other in disbelief.

"He has some questions to answer before I decide how we proceed."

The grip on Toby's wrist loosened and so did the knot in his stomach. He drew in and released his first full breath since hearing the senator's voice in the hallway. He pushed up from his sprawled position and straightened his shirt. The senator's shirt. The tie might as well have been a noose. He was going to hang for this.

"Ahem." *Breathe.* "Ahem. Senator, I know this looks really bad, and you are absolutely right in assuming I shouldn't be in here. But I didn't come into your private study to do you harm. I came in here, hoping to save my job." And now that he'd vocalized the motivation for even considering something so wrong, he wasn't sure he should offer any more excuses. He'd done this for selfish reasons. Ivan had wanted to blackmail the senator. And he had wanted to use the same information to protect his job by hoping to find something to use to blackmail Ivan.

Gina was right. All he ever thought about was how to get ahead in his job. Not the impact his drive to succeed or the choices he made had on other people. "My boss has a near obsession with you and that little notebook. He said that if I didn't find a way to get the information inside it for him, he was going to ruin me—and my career."

"So you *were* stealing it." Not a question, a logical assumption. But the choice of descriptor for his action didn't paint any softness, any sympathy, on what he was doing.

"Not steal it. I just wanted to see what the big secret was. I wanted to know what the contents were and use that information to save my job."

"Well?"

Toby's gaze snapped up from the carpet where he'd been studying his shoes, deciding his honor and integrity had fallen down somewhere below the padding underneath the rug on the floor. "I'm sorry, sir. I don't know what you mean."

"What did you see?" The senator came around the desk and sat down in his chair. He motioned Toby and Dekker to the two high-backed seats facing him.

He scooted his chair a little to the right, away from Dekker and the side of his jacket he had been reaching into before that wrist-twisting move. "That's just it. I didn't see anything. I had just opened the book when I heard you outside the door. I was putting it back."

Dekker snorted and shifted in his seat but said nothing.

The senator leaned forward and pinned Toby in place with a hard glare. "Why should I believe you?"

He couldn't do this sitting down. He'd answer all the questions they had for him and accept whatever punishment they chose to impart, but he couldn't sit motionless in that chair with all the sparks of fear and regret and recrimination zapping through his system. He'd implode. "Sir, there isn't a reason in the world for you to believe anything I've said to you. I came into your home knowing what my boss wanted me to do. A small part of why I came here tonight was for a chance to see what was in that notebook. But, I've been praying and asking God to show me what to do because I knew it was wrong when Ivan told me I had to get the book or lose my job—my reputation. I talked to Pastor Walker. I asked for his advice."

The senator went to rise from his seat and Toby motioned him back down. "I didn't give Jeremy the specifics, but he knew it involved someone influential and that Gina could be hurt by my actions."

"Gina? Abby and Katherine's friend? What does she have to do with this? Is that why she brings you to all these social functions? Is she helping you?"

"No!" The roar of his denial echoed in the silent room. "No, sir. Gina lectures me in the car all the way to any of these functions. I'm not allowed to ask leading questions. I can't take notes of any kind. I can't try to network and ask for an interview at a later date." He ran his hand through the front of his hair, knocking it clear of his eyes. "I can't be a reporter when I'm at a social gathering with her."

"But you're using her. Was that your idea or your boss's?"

The bold truth froze Toby's heart. He wanted Dekker to handcuff him and haul him out the back way so that Gina would never find out what he'd done. What Ivan had told him to do to get the story on these people, her friends. "My boss has always encouraged me to maintain a connection with Gina so that I'd have access to Pemberly's elite political figures."

"I'm sure that will warm her heart when she hears it."

"No, sir. It will turn it to ice at the mention of my name. And it should."

Just then, there was a soft tap on the study door and it opened.

"Oh, excuse me. I'm looking for Toby..." Gina's words trailed off and she bit her lower lip as all three men swung their gazes toward her. She hesitated before stepping further into the room. "I'm sorry to intrude."

Toby came toward her, his brow creased in concern and his hair a bigger mess than usual. "What's wrong?" He took her hands and squeezed gently.

"Gigi. My mother called and said they had to rush Gigi to the hospital. Frannie can't leave because of the party, but I—"

"I'll take you." He glanced back at the senator. "Sir, if you'll let me, I need to take Gina to her family. She needs to be with them. I'll return whenever you want me to and we can continue this. I'll tell you everything."

Something about the scene didn't seem right, but Gina was so anxious about Gigi that she didn't grab Toby's arm and demand that he explain what he was doing in a room with Senator Blackmon and a federal marshal looking as if he'd just been stretched over a rack. Instead, she held on to his arm for support. The muscles tightened under her hand, turning to sinewy cords of steel. Her nerves were a wreck if she was thinking Toby the Reporter and the word *steel* and flashing images of the Man of Steel. He was no Clark Kent. But he was her ride to the hospital. She had to make sure Gigi was okay. She'd promised Frannie she'd call her as soon as she got there.

"Miss Lawson, Gina." The senator rose from his desk. "If you'd like your sister to go with you, Abby and Katherine can take over with the party."

She smiled and shook her head. "Thank you, sir, but no. Frannie doesn't handle sitting and waiting very well, so she'd just be in the way. Here, she'll have something to do. I'll keep her updated." She looked between the harsh lines of Dekker's tight jaw and the senator's dark expression, then at Toby. What had he done? If he'd been trying to work a story while in the senator's home, on his birthday and New Year's Eve, she was going to borrow a carving fork from Frannie and skewer him. She'd just have to get the scoop on the way to the hospital.

Toby put his arm around her waist and pulled her closer. "Please, sir. Let me get Gina settled at the hospital with her family. Dekker can come with us and bring me back here."

What? She didn't have time for this. She'd borrow Katherine's car. It would be faster.

The senator held up his hand. "Hendricks, be here at ten in the morning. And plan on spending most of the day."

Toby acknowledged the command with a stiff nod before hustling her out of the room. He walked quickly toward the front of the house, only pausing long enough for Jeremy to hand him his jacket and her coat. He pushed the coat up her arms as soon as she straightened them and then they were outside in the biting cold walking toward his truck where the valet had it waiting.

He tipped the guy and took over helping her into the vehicle. "All set?"

He didn't wait for an affirmative before the door was closed and he was coming around and getting in on the driver's side.

"Toby, what was going on back there? What did I interrupt?"

The truck growled into gear as he shifted and released the clutch, checking traffic before pulling out onto the main road. The hospital was out near Sunny Days, so he had almost twenty minutes to explain what he had been doing.

"Nothing. We hadn't really started our discussion. I'll fill you in after it's all settled. Tell me what happened to your grandmother."

Gina wanted to argue, but keeping her worry over Gigi under control was taking all her energy. "Momma called Frannie's phone when I didn't answer." She fumbled with the sparkly device she held in a death grip. "I'd left mine in my coat pocket. Anyway, after dinner tonight, Gigi was feeling light-headed. The attendant at Sunny Days noticed and caught her before she fell. Dr. Jacobs was already at the hospital with another patient, so he told them to send an ambulance."

The phone vibrated in her hand. She swiped her finger across the screen and answered. "Momma, do they know anything more?"

"They're running some tests. Her blood pressure is fine but she's hooked up to all kinds of machines. Are you on your way?"

"Yes. Toby and I will be there in…" She glanced at him. The lights of oncoming traffic highlighted the intensity of his features.

"Less than fifteen minutes."

"I'll be there in no time. Which floor are you on?"

"We're still in the ER. Gary is sitting with your father until you get here. He didn't want Elise and the baby out in this weather. You be careful. Tell Toby not to drive too fast. Mom's stable, we just don't know what's happened to make her so dizzy."

"Okay. We'll be there soon."

"Is Frannie upset she had to stay?"

"She's fine. I promised to call her with news."

Toby sped up to beat a yellow light and a car horn honked. "Don't you dare get us into a wreck."

"We would have ended up stopped in the middle of the intersection if I'd tried to stop for that light. We were too close. And I made sure nothing was coming. I wouldn't do that to you. Not when I'm trying to get you to your grandmother."

"I'm sorry, I just. Gigi is…"

He reached over and squeezed her hand, easing

his fingers between hers. "I know. I feel the same way about Pops." He pressed his lips to the tips of her fingers. Then, keeping a loose grasp on her hand, he rested it on the seat between them and didn't let go.

Chapter 7

Gina was out of the truck before Toby could come to a full stop. He'd pulled up close to the main entrance.

"Go inside and find your family. I'll find a parking space and be right behind you."

She tried to smile but couldn't imagine what look was on her face. Her fingers still tingled where his lips had grazed them. Why did he have to become so not-Toby right now? She didn't know what to do with his solicitude. As if she wasn't wound up enough worrying about Gigi, he had to pull out his gentlemen's handbook and start practicing chivalry. She did not have time to play the damsel in distress to his knight in shining armor.

Inside the waiting area of the emergency room, Gina rushed to her father. "How is she? What happened? Who was with her?"

Her father wrapped her in his arms, trapping her hands between them—stilling them. "Take a breath. Just breathe, Gina. They were having a party in the solarium. She had been visiting with friends when she said she felt sick to her stomach. When she tried to get up, the room whirled. There was an attendant close by. He caught her before she fell and bumped her head."

She pushed away from him. "Did she pass out?"

"We're not sure. Dr. Jacobs called and spoke to the attendant and got more details about how she was before the EMTs arrived. He said it could be as simple as she just stood up too quickly, or she could have vertigo, or even an ear infection. Her heart rate and blood pressure are a little low, but not too much below average. I'm sure she's going to be fine. I told your mother not to call you and disturb the party."

"What? How could you even think of suggesting that? Can I go back and see her?"

Daddy laughed. Laughed at her. Just then, Toby came in. He paused as if unsure of his welcome into their little group. She was unsure, too. Usually Toby was the one in need of a good fussing at, but her father was still grinning and looking a little too interested in the guy standing there in a crisp white dress shirt underneath his dark jacket.

He needed a haircut and a shave. For all she knew he had some disfiguring scar underneath all that stubble. But he'd pushed his hair out of his eyes and the clear blue, almost silver of them, was piercing. And he was watching her, concerned. She'd never seen Toby Hendricks concerned about anyone but himself. Except maybe his grandfather.

"Daddy, this is my friend Toby. Toby, this is my father, George."

He reached out his hand. "Nice to meet you, sir."

Her father pumped his hand and smiled. "I read your column in the *Sentinel* every day. Is that how you two met? Were you covering some political story and ran into my Gina with her fancy friends?"

"Daddy, stop."

The security doors leading to the patient area opened and Gary walked through. Gina chewed her lower lip. Toby stepped up beside her and clasped her hand in his, holding it tight until Gary reached to hug her.

"She's fine, Gina. They're waiting on a few more test results, but they may let her go home tonight."

"Do they know what caused the dizziness?"

"A little too much sugar, not enough rest today, and she forgot she was an old lady and jumped up too quick. She still has some nausea and a headache. The doctor is trying to decide whether she has an ear infection. Her white cell count is up and so is her sugar. He's waiting on the ENT specialist to see her and he wants to make sure the dizziness has stopped before he releases her."

"Can I see her?"

"Yeah, sure. That's why I came out. Mom said you should be here by now."

"Okay, give me a minute." She turned and walked with Toby toward the entrance.

"Do you want me to stay while you go make sure she's all right?"

She looked up and met his tender gaze. "No, but

thank you. My family's here so I have a ride home. I appreciate you driving me."

"Hey." He caught her chin with his fingers and turned her face back to him. "I'm not trying to get you off my hands so I can take off. I want to make sure you have what you need. I'm here—for you."

She ran her teeth over her lower lip, her heart warmed by his words. "I didn't think you knew how to do that."

He smiled and tapped his index finger against her nose. "I didn't either, but you're special. I care…"

His gaze drifted away and he cleared his throat before making eye contact again. She rose up on her tiptoes, holding on to the edges of his jacket and kissed his scratchy cheek. The stubble was actually softer than she'd expected. "Thank you."

He pressed his lips to her forehead and held her tight for the span of several of his steady heartbeats. "I'm sorry."

She looked up. He stepped back and turned. The swish of the doors and the cold claimed him.

Toby drove home from the hospital with the sweet, spicy scent of Gina's hair overloading his senses. He prayed for her and for her grandmother. Her brother's comments made it sound as if everything was fine, but he may have been downplaying the seriousness of the situation so Gina wouldn't be alarmed.

He couldn't count the times he'd downplayed something to keep from upsetting Gina, but that was usually for self-preservation. Her family's efforts were meant for her. And tonight so were his. And he realized the truth in his heart. Oh, he was so messed up.

Why would God pick now to have all this come together in his life? This wasn't part of his five-year plan. He wasn't ever supposed to have to choose right over wrong. And choosing right shouldn't end up costing him everything.

Pastor Walker had encouraged him to trust God. He had. Hadn't he? He looked at the clock. If it weren't so late, he'd go see Pops and ask for a little guidance. But it was one minute till midnight. He waited for it. Happy New Year. But not for him.

He drove home and let himself into his apartment with a sense of isolation so thick and unbreachable, he could have been the last man on earth. And in a way, he was. Out with the old, in with the new. His whole life was gone. He'd lost it all.

Pops had given him his study Bible, the one with tiny print, when he found out Toby had been to church a couple of times. According to Pops, he wasn't supposed to just read the Word during services—he was supposed to read it daily.

Pops, I'm not even sure God can get me out of the mess I'm in now.

The Bible was right where he'd put it when he brought it home. On his nightstand, beside his bed. He'd figured he could use it as a sleep aid if he was having trouble sleeping. But he wouldn't be sleeping tonight no matter what he tried. His future was gone. His plans to become the best journalist Pemberly had ever seen, and therefore to get out of Pemberly, had crashed and burned.

Pops would probably believe him when he explained what had happened. Gina, though. If he could write in every language known to man, he still wouldn't be able to write an explanation that would earn him her forgiveness—her restored favor.

And that was the shocking truth he was struggling to understand tonight. Of everything, even the fear of going to jail, which could happen in the morning if the senator wanted it to, nothing compared to the pain he knew his actions, his compromises for the sake of his career, would cause Gina when she learned the truth. And she'd hear the story. There was no way Abby or Katherine wouldn't tell her.

She might not love him like he— *Whoa. Not going to finish that thought. Can't finish it. That chance is gone, too.*

He scrubbed his hands over his face. What was he thinking? His stomach cramped and he fought the shock of truth that had just blindsided him. Love and commitment didn't have a place in his life!

But nothing else was going according to plan, so why should his heart cooperate? It wanted Gina no matter what it cost him. It ached for her. He taunted her into squabbling with him because she was never more beautiful than when she had a spark of temper in her eyes and that cocky chin was notched up at him, ready to do battle. But he'd made one too many bad choices and now there would be no getting back what he'd lost.

He sat down on the bed and opened the Bible to one of the bookmarks Pops had left between the pages. First 1 John 2:17. *And the world passeth away, and the lust thereof: but he that doeth the will of God abideth forever.*

Even God saw fit to confirm his belief that everything was gone. Passed away. Well, today was the first day of the rest of his life, as the saying went. He closed his eyes and asked God to help him do His will because he had definitely messed things up trying to do his own.

The hours on the clock ticked by as he switched his focus from counting the minutes to thumbing through and reading various Scriptures as the sun rose and climbed higher in the sky on its way to ten in the morning.

At nine, he stood in the shower, letting the heat of the water help cleanse his body of the aches of his past. Whatever happened with the senator, he would do what God showed him was right. Ivan had stolen the last piece of his soul he would ever get.

He debated whether to shave or not, but in the end he remembered one of the old hymns they used to sing whenever he'd gone to church with his grandparents. "Just As I Am." That's how he'd present himself today to the senator and Dekker, US marshal. His stomach tensed and he wondered if what they had given Gina's grandmother for nausea was available over the counter.

The drive to the senator's house took less time than it should considering how law-abiding he'd kept his speed through town. There was enough trouble waiting for him at the Blackmon residence.

Toby checked his phone after he pulled up in front of one of the closed garage doors at the senator's home. He'd turned it off before walking into the ER last night and since the only person likely to contact him was Ivan demanding a status report, he'd left it off.

There were thirty text messages from Ivan. Those

might come in handy depending on what was waiting for him inside. There was one from Gina early this morning. Gigi was at Gina's parents' house and doing fine. She would stay there for a couple of days until her follow-up appointment with Dr. Jacobs. Good. God had answered that prayer with no trouble. But then it had been for someone else. He'd have to wait and see how things went in regard to the prayers he'd sent up for himself last night.

Dekker opened the door. Anytime Toby came into contact with the man, it always threw him off balance. He understood how the world worked and who were the movers and shakers. He understood that Senator Blackmon was a powerful man. But Toby had never put him high above everyone else because that wasn't how the senator treated people. He didn't parade around as if he was draped in a purple robe and wearing a crown. When he had a conversation with anyone, he spoke earnestly and listened intently. Toby prayed he would do that with him this morning.

"Follow me." Dekker didn't wait to see if he obeyed, just headed down that same hallway Toby had on his way to the bathroom.

Dekker held the door for Toby to precede him into the study. The senator was seated behind his desk. A movement to his left caught his attention. Jeremy Walker was standing in front of an oxblood leather love seat. His eyes weren't hard, but his expression wasn't welcoming either.

Toby nodded toward him. "Pastor Walker."

"Toby."

The soft click of the door closing twisted the knot

in the pit of Toby's stomach a little tighter. He closed his eyes and asked God to be with him.

Dekker went around behind the desk and stood at the senator's shoulder. The pastor took Dekker's seat from the night before, leaving Toby only one seating option. If that was the only choice taken from him today, he would count it a huge win.

"Have a seat, Toby. It's time we got to the bottom of this mess." The senator leaned back and opened the middle drawer on his desk. He took the notebook out and dropped it in the center of his desk.

"What do you want to know?" Toby asked.

"All of it. Down to what your boss said about why he has it in for me."

Toby shook his head. "*Why* is the one thing I can't tell you. When I asked, he told me it wasn't any of my business. That's why I was in here looking for the notebook. I hoped its contents would shed some light on Ivan's motivations, but like I told you last night, I had just taken it out of the drawer when I heard you and Dekker in the hall. I was putting it back, without reading it, when you caught me."

"Toby, this is what you were asking my advice about, isn't it?" The pastor's voice remained neutral.

He bobbed his head up and down. "Ivan had just issued his threat and I was shell-shocked. I didn't know where to go or what to do. I climbed in my truck and drove. Grace Community Church was directly in front of me. I took it as a sign that God knew what was happening and was going to help me."

"Did he?"

Toby met the minister's direct gaze. "That's the thing. There were times when things were happening and I was sure the problem was solved. Then Ivan would corner me and ask how I planned to get my hands on it." His eyes strayed to the leather notebook that had started all this craziness. "I know how everyone sees me. I'm the guy hanging around, waiting for something to happen or for one of you to let go of a big secret so I can make headline news. I'll push until I get the truth if I know there's more going on than people are saying. But, I don't break the law to get information and I've been friends with Gina because I like her, not because my boss told me to use her connections with all of you."

The senator shifted in his chair. "If you don't agree with Ivan's methods, why are you working for him?"

"He's only been with the *Sentinel* for a couple of years. He transferred in as managing editor from a smaller paper when Mr. Grainger retired. I had just started writing features when he arrived. His style of reporting and mine didn't mesh, so he edited my work with a heavy hand for the first few months. After that, he assigned me to some of the local political beats and encouraged me to find out the truth no matter how hard I had to push."

"I see he hasn't changed in all these years." The senator sat back and steepled his fingers together.

"You know Ivan Strong? But he's never worked in Washington."

"It wasn't a pleasant encounter and it was many years ago. Does he still have the gold tooth?"

"Yes, sir.

"I want you to tell me exactly what Ivan Strong ordered you to do and what he threatened to do to you if you didn't carry out his demands."

Toby wiped his sweaty palms on the legs of his jeans. "He showed me some news clips of you taking the notebook out and scribbling something in it after whoever you were speaking with had walked away. He is convinced that book holds all kinds of incriminating secrets that you use against people to gain their votes."

The senator shook his head. "He's only gotten worse over the years."

"He's the photographer, isn't he?" This was the first time Jeremy had spoken since Toby began recounting his story. And this question wasn't for Toby. Jeremy was looking at the senator.

"Yes, he is. I paid for that shiny tooth of his many years ago."

"Wha—"

He dismissed Toby's question with a wave of his hand. "Ancient history. Tell me what he threatened to do to you."

"He said if I didn't either take the notebook or make a copy of its contents, he was going to fire me. After that, he was going to run a final article under my name, filled with false or plagiarized information." Toby swallowed hard against the fury burning its way up into the back of his throat. "He said I'd never work for another newspaper in the Southeast again. And if he carries out his threat, he's right. It would take me years to clear my name, and even if I could prove I didn't write the article, once it goes live, it's out there forever. I'd lose all credibility."

"And yet you considered doing it to get ahead."

The burn of shame replaced the heat of fury inside him. "Yes, I did."

The silence stretched as the senator's gaze held his. Toby was powerless to look away. Whatever this man decided as his fate, he deserved. He'd always heard the saying "an eye for an eye." By trying to stand on his own ambition, he'd betrayed his principles. Pops had set the foundation for his sense of right and wrong when he was a little boy spending summers with his grandparents. And during the talks they had now over sandwich cookies and milk.

This was his day of reckoning for turning his back on what was right. God knew what he'd done. And soon, so would Pops and Gina. He'd be leaving Pemberly. There was no way he could look them or any of the other residents of this town in the eye after today.

The senator held the little notebook up in his hand. "So, you sacrificed your career, your good name, your honor for this book without knowing what it was or what it contained. Am I right?"

He nodded.

"Then you'd still do what Ivan wanted in order to keep your job."

"No. It was wrong of him to ask me to do it and it was even worse for me to entertain the idea of doing it, even for a second. I'm as guilty as if I had handed the book over to him."

"I'm not going to let you hand it over to him. But I am going to let you read enough of what's on the pages inside to write an accurate story. And I get to be your editor."

"What? Sir, I don't—"

"No, Toby Hendricks, *you* don't. I do. This is my bargain with you. I'll let you read what's in here, but you have to write the complete truth about what you find. You can't use names and I'm pretty sure I didn't list any, but still, no names in the article but yours and mine. And you'll include why you're writing this story. Or..."

Toby was trying to get his jaw to move so he could close his mouth. After all this regret and turmoil he'd been wrestling with for the past month, the senator was handing him the notebook. And demanding he write the article. Had he stepped into the Twilight Zone?

"Or, you find another career."

The same choices Ivan had given him but entirely different. "I don't understand."

"Ivan was willing to risk your future on the unknown contents of this book. I'm asking if you are willing to do the same." He waved the book in front of Toby again. "This could be my grocery list, the codes to a secret bank account or something entirely different. Choose. Now."

He let out a long breath. "It's the same as before. I don't really have a choice. If I write the story, Ivan won't let me include the part about him coercing me into taking the book. And once I confess to considering doing it, no one will respect me or trust what I write again. If I don't write the story, he'll ruin my name with a bogus article and I'll still lose my credibility, my reputation." For the first time since he sat down, Toby's eyes cut to Dekker, still standing silent and threatening. Like a sentinel. This meeting grew more ironic by the minute. "And that doesn't include the punishment I'll receive after my conviction."

"Your conviction? Are you going to jail?" Dekker's voice was taunting.

"Whether I was going to take the book or not, you caught me, literally red-handed. That's attempted theft and breaking and entering."

The senator pitched the book at him. Toby caught it in a fumbling effort.

"I want your word that you will force Ivan Strong to run the article you write about the contents of that book."

"But—"

"Your word, Mr. Hendricks. And a truthful article about what's inside that book. You know your other option."

"Why? Why are you insisting I divulge your secrets? Are you going to sue the *Sentinel* after the story runs? Ivan and I are the only two people who did anything wrong here. If you sue the paper, you'd win because writing that article would defame you. The paper could close. The other people working there didn't do anything wrong. They don't deserve to lose their jobs."

The senator leaned forward, his arms folded in front of him on the desk. "Say yes and open the book, Toby."

"I have no choice."

"Open the book."

He prayed, asking God for His forgiveness and His help. But unless an earthquake happened in the next second, Toby was committed to the path Ivan had paved—no, he and Ivan had paved for him.

The inside cover was embossed with a Scripture. Toby's eyes shot to the senator.

"Read it aloud."

"'For I say, through the grace given unto me, to

every man that is among you, not to think of himself more highly than he ought to think; but to think soberly, according as God hath dealt to every man the measure of faith. Romans twelve, three.'"

His eyes skimmed the first page of notations. He flipped the page and did the same. "Bob's mother. Abby and Jeremy. The hurricane victims. The veterans. The Senate. Congress. The President. The servicemen and -women." On and on it went, a list of people or groups of people. Sometimes there was an extra word or two. "Cancer. Death. Car accident. New job. Broken arm."

"What is this?"

"It's a prayer journal. A yearly gift from my wife. With my job, I meet a lot of people every day. And most of them have a need for prayer. I know I don't have to name them individually because God knows the needs of us all, but still, I feel better if I can be specific enough to at least say their names when I ask God's hand on their lives. With so much information coming into my brain, I worry someone's name or need will be pushed out or buried under the new stuff. The journal is a visual prompt of what I need to pray about that day. The Scripture is to remind me that though I hold a position of authority, of power, in our country, I'm not better than the people I represent. I'm one of them. As flawed and as forgiven as the next man. As you."

Pastor Walker clapped his hand on Toby's shoulder. "I told you God would be there waiting when you tried to find your way back onto the right path."

"Yeah, you did. I don't think I fully understood what you meant at the time." Toby turned his attention

back to the senator. "I will be happy to write the article. And I have no problem threatening to quit if Ivan
refuses to run it or wants to change it. In fact, if he
does, I'll call a friend who works at an Atlanta paper
and ask if they will run it as a guest columnist feature.
The fact that you're a senator would get it printed in
just about any paper within your constituency."

"I want to see the article before you turn it in and
I want a printed copy that is signed and witnessed on
every page for my records."

Toby shook his head. "I keep forgetting that most
of the people I've met through Gina are attorneys.
You all do like a paper trail."

"Physical proof has exonerated as many as it has
convicted. And I'm old-fashioned. I like having something permanent in my hands."

He hated to ask, but he had to know. "What about
Ivan?"

Dekker relaxed his military stance and an unset-
tling smile raised his lips. "You write your story, Hendricks. I'll deal with Strong." After a brief dip of his
head to the senator, he was gone.

The senator and Jeremy rose from their seats,
prompting Toby to do the same. The senator came
around the desk and offered his hand. "Go write your
article. Call me when you're ready for me to read it."

"What about my job?"

"You are working. On the assignment you were
given. Call Ivan and tell him you need the extra time
off to get it right. All will be well."

It wasn't that simple. There were too many things
left unsettled, but he was walking out of this room
with a clear conscience and a chance at a new start.

He'd trusted this meeting to God and God had taken care of it. Just like Jeremy had said He would. When he'd realized he was on the wrong track, God had given him the compass to get back to where he should be.

On her way to work, Gina stopped at the local bookstore and bought five copies of the morning edition of the *Sentinel*. She didn't know what she was going to do with the extra copies. She only planned to have one framed as a gift to Toby.

His feature spread on Senator Blackmon and his prayer journal had brought tears to her eyes. She'd been praying and praying ever since she had met him and he'd made his first snarky comment about church and God, asking the Lord to open his eyes and his heart to the truth of God's love. A man who didn't know God couldn't have written that story. It was a beautiful tribute to faithfulness and humility. She had worried she would never be able to use those two character traits to describe Toby.

Something had happened on New Year's Eve to change him—them. He'd been kind, and concerned. Tender. He'd teased her when he called her yesterday, checking on her grandmother's recuperation. He was different. Not as intense about his job. It was as if he were at peace.

Whatever it was, somewhere deep inside, it scared her a little. There was nothing lovable about the snarly Toby. This tender version could be heart-melting if she wasn't careful. He hadn't mentioned his big five-year plan in the past few days, but she knew he wanted to escape Pemberly for a bigger paper and a bigger byline. Falling for Toby model 2.0 didn't offer any more of a future than the original design. Her future lay in Pemberly, near her family. His did not.

Katherine and Nick had taken the week off. Her morning sickness hadn't improved and Nick wanted her to rest. The only way to keep Katherine from working was to hold her hostage at some remote vacation spot. The Blackmons owned a cabin in the mountains that boasted no cell reception. If Nick wanted to isolate her, that was the best place to keep her. So Gina had forwarded Katherine's office phones to Abby's office and was working from there all week.

A deliveryman arrived midmorning with a cookie bouquet. Toby had remembered she was allergic to flowers. After the invasion of rose petals during Nick's courtship of Katherine, every drug store in town knew about her allergy. She'd bought out their entire stock of Benadryl.

Another delivery came after lunch. It was a large box from a high-end gift store specializing in crystal. Wrapped in yards of bubble wrap, buried under a pile of packing peanuts, was a smaller box.

Abby walked in as she was brushing off any clinging peanuts. "Do you have a secret admirer?"

"He isn't including a card, but I'm pretty sure they're all from Toby." She couldn't have stopped the smile from spreading across her face any more than she could have slowed the warmth spreading through her chest to her heart.

But Abby's response wasn't as happy.

"What is it?"

Abby shook her head and looked toward the ceiling. 'I promised Jeremy I wouldn't get involved, but I can't let him do this to you."

"Who? Jeremy? What would he do to me?"

"Not Jeremy. Toby." Abby folded her arms across her middle.

"If you know something about Toby that involves me, you need to tell me." She looked up and met Abby's troubled eyes with a direct look. "I would tell you."

With a loud huff and a growl, Abby sat down in the chair across from Gina. "Fine. But I'm not telling you this to hurt your feelings. It's because you need to know what Toby's been doing—to you."

Dread seized Gina's insides, its cold fingers reaching out and chilling her to her soul. "What's he been doing?"

"His boss. Or rather, his former boss thanks to Daddy, told him to get close to you. To use your friendships with Katherine and me to get information on Daddy, Nick and even Jeremy." She reached out and took Gina's hand in a warm grasp. "Gina, he's been using you for the chance at a big story because his boss told him to do it. He came to the party as a cover so he could break into Daddy's study and steal his prayer journal because his boss wanted it. They didn't even know what it was."

The ice that had seized her heart at the beginning of Abby's revelation vaporized. The heat of her anger, her disgust, incinerated any kindness she's assigned to his name. She shoved the unopened gift box into the garbage can. The sound of breaking glass shattered the silence of the room.

The gifts, his kindness to her at the hospital all

made sense now. She'd rescued him from his punishment. She'd have been grateful, too. Her eyes dropped to the five copies of the newspaper. She tossed them into the garbage on top of the other box.

"Gina, I didn't tell you this to upset you. I told you to warn you. I'm so sorry. I wish it weren't true. More than you know." She came around the desk and caught Gina in a fierce hug. "I'm so sorry."

Gina freed herself from Abby's embrace. "It's okay. I've always known the reason he hung around was my connection to all of y'all. He was nice to me the night my grandmother got sick. I see now it had nothing to do with my concern for her. I helped him delay his reckoning with your father." She took her purse out of the bottom drawer of her desk. "At least he's consistent. But then, that was part of his plan all along." She dug her keys out of the side pocket of her bag, then straightened the strap on her shoulder. "If you'll excuse me, I need to take an early lunch."

"Yes, of course. Gina, I—"

"Don't, Abby. Please don't pity me. This is my fault. I liked arguing with him. It kept me from being bored while I waited for God to send me my soul mate. I guess I was the one providing the entertainment." She left the office before Abby could see just how much hurt Toby had inflicted. She didn't even want to lash out at him. That would be too much like their sparring matches when she'd believed he liked her, maybe even respected her. She might be a fool. But she wasn't going to be a crybaby. Not over Toby Hendricks.

Chapter 8

Gigi was still staying with Gina's parents. Gina drove there and let herself inside. She followed the rapid clack of knitting needles into the family room. Gigi was sitting in an overstuffed chair with her feet propped up on the ottoman.

"Gina, sweetie, what are you doing home in the middle of the day?"

She hurried to her grandmother and dropped to her knees. Gigi shoved her knitting away and wrapped her in her loving arms. "Honey, what is it?"

She shook her head, not able to tell her grandmother how stupid, how gullible she'd been. Gigi held her. Rubbing her back and playing with her curls, letting Gina cry until there were no tears left. No pressure, no judgment. Just love and acceptance, which made her want to start bawling all over again.

Her head hurt and her temper was brewing like a boiling pot left on the stove too long. "The reporter I thought was my friend was only trying to get a story from my real friends."

"I see. Did he use you to get the story that ran in today's paper about the senator's prayer journal?"

Gina nodded. "Worse, he used my invitation to the senator's birthday party to try and steal it. Momma called about you being taken to the hospital and I went looking for him. I interrupted the senator and a US marshal who had caught him in the act. He used driving me to the hospital as an excuse to get away from them." She pounded her fist on the cushioned arm of the chair. "I was so stupid. I knew I shouldn't trust him, but I liked him. I teased him about using me for my connections." She leaned back on her feet. "I guess the joke's on me, huh?"

"No, honey. Your intentions were honorable."

"No, Gigi, they weren't. I liked fighting with him. I insulted him and thrived on beating him. I see now that wasn't nice. Teasing is one thing, but I would get caught up in the game and I wasn't kind." She kept her head down, not able to face the look of censure in Gigi's eyes.

But Gigi was having none of it. She cupped Gina's face in her hands and drew her head up until their eyes met. There was nothing sterner than gentle admonishment and nothing warmer than the love of a grandmother looking upon her cherished grandchild. "You need to talk to him. Give him a chance to explain."

Before Gina could shake her head in denial, Gigi squeezed her cheeks. "Uh-huh. If you don't confront him, this anger and disappointment will grow until it takes over the spaces in your heart reserved for love. Even if you can't mend your relationship, you won't be able to move forward with all this stirring in you. You won't be able to let go of the distrust for him in order to trust another. Don't give his actions more power to affect you than they already have."

"How did you get to be so wise?"

"Years and years with your poppy, darling. Now, go wash your face. You have some raking to do."

Gina was uncrouching from her awkward position. She stopped, teetering on the balls of her feet. "Raking?"

"You do intend to rake him over the coals for his awful behavior? You'd better. No granddaughter of mine would let a man get away with such bad behavior. Now, go. Clean your face and then take him to task."

"I love you, Gigi." She hugged her grandmother tight.

"Of course. What's not to love?"

Gina went upstairs to the bathroom. She blotted her eyes with a cool cloth and touched up her makeup by dusting powder across her Rudolph-red nose. She didn't want to take the time to assess what crying her heart out over Toby Hendricks implied. She'd told him she didn't think she could forgive dishonesty. And after being on the receiving of his perfidy, she was positive she couldn't. Now to get through severing all ties with him without letting him see her shed a tear.

She used her anger at him, and herself, to feed her temper as she drove to his office. She was too smart, too suspicious for him to have so thoroughly duped her. Him and his puppy-dog eyes and scruffy looks. He was about to get his ears trimmed.

Visitor parking for the *Sentinel* was on the street. There was a sign with an arrow labeled Employee Parking that pointed to the parking garage behind the building. A man coming through the glass doors that opened onto the street held one open for her as she approached and didn't seem to see anything amiss. Apparently, the dusting of powder she'd applied had done a good job at masking the ravages of disillusionment. She smiled her thanks and stepped inside.

The elevators were straight across the lobby. She walked with purpose—definite purpose. The heels of her suede boots tapped out her intent on the tiled floor. She pushed the call button. When the doors opened, Toby halted midstride, his foot dangling over the threshold.

"Gina."

"Scumbag." She grabbed hold of his jacket and snatched him into the lobby before the doors closed and he escaped.

"Gina, it isn't what you think." He tried to pry her fingers loose.

"Why don't you tell me what it isn't?" She kept walking, dragging him with her by the handful of his jacket caught in her fist.

Another man coming into the building held the door for her this time. She offered him a grateful smile. "Thank you very much."

Toby sputtered and dragged his feet, trying either to stop her or get free. She wasn't sure which and she didn't really care. It would be better to do this in private, but out on the street for all of Pemberly to see was just as well. That way she wouldn't have to re-count the ugliness to everyone. The gossips would take care of sharing the gory details for her.

Outside and two blocks down from the glass-encased building the *Sentinel* called home, she aimed for the park and the ornate concrete bridge that arched over a dry creek.

"Gina, let go of me."

Like he had a say in this. But he was pulling back while she was tugging forward. She let go. He stag-gered backward and came to an abrupt stop against the side of the bridge.

"Ow! What'd you do that for?" He rubbed at his elbow. A chipped funny bone would be the least of his worries.

"Consider that a practice hit." She stepped into his space, the toe of her boots bumping against his leather boat shoes.

"Tell me what you know?"

"Uh-uh. I've shared all the information I'm going to with you." She could have scratched his eyes out, she was so angry. So humiliated. So hurt. She hadn't wanted to give him her heart and then he stole it any-way. But after he'd stomped all over it, she wasn't going to let him keep it.

"Will you let me explain?" He wasn't defensive and snarling. He was—resigned.

"You can try. Not that I will ever believe another word that comes out of your mouth or I see printed in a newspaper."

"Who told you?"

"How does that matter?"

"I need to know where to start with my explanation."

"Don't you mean excuses?"

He grasped her arms at the triceps. She wasn't sure if it was to keep her from walking away or from whacking him with her purse. She still had her feet. One high heel strategically planted across the top of his foot and he would be on the ground crying like... Well, the way she had earlier.

"Just listen, please. Hear me out. If you don't believe what I tell you, then you can walk away and I'll never bother you again."

"I would think that's what you want anyway."

He caught her lips between his fingers and held them shut with gentle pressure. "Let me explain."

She bristled. He'd never taken that managing tone with her before. But she nodded her assent. Might as well let him give her his sob story so she wouldn't have to wonder why he'd used her.

He brushed a cluster of curls away from her face, tucking them behind her ear. "My boss, Ivan, has a grudge against Senator Blackmon. It goes back to when Abby was a teenager and she broke his camera with some sort of martial arts kick. That's how he got that creepy gold tooth. He lost a tooth in a scuffle with the senator. Instead of making a big deal about it, Blackmon bought him a fancier camera and paid for his dental work. Ivan had the dentist use the most expensive cap. Never mind that it makes him look like some evil minion out of an old horror movie."

She tried to speak, but he rested a finger against her lips. "Listen to me.

"He was convinced the notebook contained damaging information he could use against the senator. He told me I had to get it for him or he would ruin me by printing false articles under my name." She sucked in a breath and he shook his head no. "I told him he was crazy and that I wouldn't do it. That's when he went into detail about just how planned out and complete my ruination would be. No one would be willing to hire me even if I could prove I didn't write the articles. My honesty would always be in question."

She quirked an eyebrow at him. "And you think it isn't now? With me?"

He shot her a weak imitation of his cocky grin. "I'm hoping. But please, let me finish." At her nod, he let out a deep sigh. "I didn't know where to go, what to do. I couldn't talk to my grandfather. I didn't want to risk him thinking I would do something like that. And then there was you."

"Me? How is this my fault?"

"Gina, hush. It wasn't your fault. I was worried about what you'd think of me. And I know. Pond scum. You made that very clear in the lobby back there. I ended up at Grace Community."

"Church. You went to see Jeremy?"

"More like God wound me up and pointed me in that direction. And yeah, I just said I willingly went to church and sought counsel from Pastor Walker. He assured me of the privacy of what we discussed. I didn't tell him Ivan was going after the senator. Just that my boss had put me in a position where I had no choice but to either quit or do something that might be against the law and was definitely unethical. He told me to pray, that God would help me. And He did."

"How? You stole the notebook. Toby, you've been

putting a spin on the truth for so long *you* don't know what's real and what you've dreamed up as justification for your actions. Did or didn't your boss tell you to become my friend?"

"He did. But—"

"There's no but here, Toby. Either you pretended to be my friend or you didn't. You've just said you did what he said. And now that I know why you were in the senator's study, I realize you used my panic over Gigi's condition to get yourself out of trouble—or at least to delay it until you could come up with one of your stories."

"That isn't what happened." He took hold of her arms again when she tried to move past him.

"Then what did? Because I'm pretty sure Dekker wanted to shoot you and I'm not sure Senator Black-mon was going to tell him not to when I walked in on your little meeting."

He let go of her arms and moved beside her, facing the opposite direction with his hands resting on the cold concrete railing of the bridge. "I had been struggling with what to do. If I went back into the office and refused to do Ivan's bidding right then, I wouldn't have a chance to find a way out of it." He shot her a stern glare. "So, I kept putting him off.

"I was praying, asking God to show me what to do. And then you invited me to the senator's house. When Ivan was pressuring me for an update, I told him I was going to the party. That bought me a couple of days. At the party, after that woman spilled her juice all over my shirt and Nick gave me directions to the bathroom, he told me it was across from the senator's study."

"It was like dangling a carrot in front of you."

"Can't you understand? I'm not any good at being good. My father taught me that you use people to better yourself. And if someone lets you use them, you do. If you don't believe any of what I've already told you, believe this. I was disgusted when Ivan demanded I steal that notebook. But the more I thought about it, the more I was curious as to what it contained. Then I reasoned that if I saw the information, maybe there was something I could use to threaten Ivan and make him leave me alone.

"You're half-right, Gina. I didn't go into Senator Blackmon's study to steal the book. I went in there to read it for my use—which makes me just as bad as Ivan. The senator came in before I had time to open it. And the main reason I didn't steal it wasn't that I knew it was wrong. It was because I was afraid of getting caught. Of shaming Pops, and of what you'd think of me."

He turned his head toward her and the lost look in his eyes shriveled the taunt on her tongue to ashes. If he was acting, he deserved an award. But he'd shaken her trust in him. She wasn't willing to tread a path that could collapse underneath her feet. And believing Toby's story was too big a hazard. He'd used her. Lied to her. And made her care about him. She wouldn't give him the power to break her, too.

"It's a nice story. Almost as touching as the one you wrote about the senator and the prayer journal. But I can't afford to believe you. Life and trust aren't part of a five-year plan. They're a commitment, a loyalty that lasts forever. And I'm a forever kind of girl. You're a short-term kind of guy. It was fun fighting with you, but then, it was all just a game, wasn't it? Congratulations, you win." She kept her eyes open against the cold sting of tears, knowing that if she blinked they'd escape and then he'd know how much he'd almost won.

He reached out and cupped her cheek. "If I won, then why does it feel like I'm losing my best friend?"

Gina flinched at the warmth of his hand against her icy cheek. It took everything she had not to turn into his warmth, but the wind whipping around them was a chilling reminder of just how cold and convincing he was when pretending he cared. "You don't have friends, just sources. And like me, they're all dried up."

Toby watched Gina go. The wind had picked up, swirling sand and leaves into the air as if ushering her away. She didn't pause or look back. She was gone. And had no reason to come back. He'd hurt her more than anyone should ever be allowed to do.

There's a payday someday. It wasn't a pretty truth to realize when the woman you loved was leaving you behind. Glad to be rid of you. But he'd created the situation that sent her away. If he'd been honest with her when they met or when they first became friends, he might have had a chance. But not now. She was really and truly gone.

The wind cut through his jacket and shirt to his skin but had little effect. He was already frozen inside. He walked back toward the street to the sidewalk. Instead of heading toward the paper, he walked in the opposite direction, going the five blocks it took to reach what was becoming his refuge. Grace Community Church.

He entered through the doors to the recreation center. The gym was unlocked. Inside, all was quiet. Sunlight glinted through short rectangular windows along the walls where they met the ceiling. A cart loaded with basketballs was pushed up against the wall underneath the scoreboard.

He was no Jeremy Walker on the court, but Toby thought he could hold his own in a game against himself. He took the shot. And missed by a mile. Big surprise there. He dribbled and tried again. The ball bounced off the rim and veered hard right.

The door clicked closed as Jeremy hustled to catch the ball. "I didn't know you played roundball."

"And you still don't." Toby caught the overarm side shot Jeremy used to return the ball. He stood in place, bouncing it with one hand and then the other.

"So, I guess this means you aren't here for a quick pickup game."

Toby stopped dribbling and propped the ball on his hip. "To be honest, I don't know why I'm here. I... Gina came to the office. She knew about the senator catching me in his study with the prayer journal. She was not happy. And now I'm not happy because she left."

"Where did she go?"

"Away from me. And she made it very clear she wants it to stay that way. So, not only have I killed my career, but I've lost my best friend." He ran his fingers through his hair, pushing it back out of his eyes. "So, except for my grandfather who lives at Sunny Days, there isn't anything keeping me in Pemberly. It might be best for everyone if I looked for a job somewhere else."

"I thought you went after truth, justice and the American way. Sorry, that's another reporter, darker hair and glasses."

"I need a spiritual guide a lot more than I do a comedian right now. And if that's your best joke, you should really stick to your day job."

"Ouch. A little prickly there, aren't you?"

Toby walked over to the players' bench and plopped down. "Pastor, I've done a lot of soul-searching during this past month. Most of it since the senator's party. Deep inside, I'm not a very good person. I'm selfish, cocky, arrogant and I had this stupid plan for my life all plotted out with little tick marks to check off each goal I achieved.

"Nowhere on that list did I include friendship for the sake of friendship and just enjoying someone else's company. There had to be an agenda, a way to use that person to advance my career. I didn't leave room for God. I weighed every person I met based on how they could help me get closer to checking off another one of my goals. That is not the heart of a good person. That's a narcissist. I'm a narcissist. And now I don't have a reason to try to be better. She's gone."

"Man, you are pathetic." Jeremy sat down beside him.

"Again, keep the day job."

"I *was* doing the day job just then."

"Oh, sorry." Toby ran his hand across the back of his neck, leaning forward with his elbows resting on his thighs.

Jeremy put his hand on Toby's shoulder, like a pastor. "Just kidding. Yes, your life is a train wreck and it's going to take time and a whole bunch of effort to clean it up and get it back to functioning at full throttle and in a better direction. But if you don't try to move that first piece of debris, overcome that first obstacle, it's going to stay a really big mess. And then the weeds will start growing, locking into place those things that it would be easy to clear away now, while they're fresh, and leaving you with an even bigger mess."

"Agghhh. You are not making me feel better. What am I supposed to do? Gina's gone. She doesn't want to hear a thing I have to say. Pops isn't going to be happy when he finds out the details about how I gained the privilege to write that article on the senator. My father is going to jump in and play devil's advocate, because really, sometimes, I think that's what he is. He is the most selfish, self-absorbed person I've ever met. And I've been just like him."

"Does your father think he's a narcissist? Does he care, much less notice, when his actions cause anyone else pain? Does he spend time with his father at Sunny Days?"

"No to all the above."

"Then you aren't your father. You aren't your grandfather either. I've met him. I just didn't make the connection. He's a good man with a strong faith. He loves to talk about you. He's a lot of fun. He and Mrs. Montego…"

"What? Are you going to give me grief over my grandfather having a lady friend, too? He chose to spend Christmas with her and her family instead of my parents. That ought to tell you how difficult it is to be around my parents."

"Have you met Mrs. Montego?"

"Yes, she's nice. She doesn't let Pops off the hook with anything. She keeps him straight." He laughed remembering some of the stern lectures his visits had interrupted. "She makes him happy. And that makes me happy."

"You should meet her granddaughter—"

"Just stop right there, Pastor. I'm sitting here telling you I've finally realized I'm in love with Gina and she doesn't want anything to do with me. You're as bad as Pops trying to set me up with a woman who spends her Saturday afternoons reading to old people. I want Gina, not the woman with no dating prospects. So please, don't try to hook me up with anyone else. All I want is Gina."

Jeremy shook his head but finally relented. "Okay, I'll leave you alone so you can wallow in your misery. Let me know when you're ready to do something about your situation." He clapped Toby on the back before pushing to his feet and heading for the door.

"Which one of my situations?"

"Any of them," Jeremy said without turning around.

Chapter 9

Toby came into the *Sentinel*'s offices early the next day with a cardboard box, ready to clean out his desk. He'd spoken to his friend at a paper in Atlanta. They had a part-time position for a movie reviewer. The satire was not lost on him. He was leaving to escape the constant reminders of Gina for a job he used to ask her to help him do. All for less pay, no benefits and higher rent. And no discussions with Gina after the chick flicks.

He sat down in his chair and let the box drop to the floor. As he pulled his bottom drawer open, he heard raised voices coming from Ivan's office. He stood up in time to see Dekker wearing a big smile as he grasped Ivan's arm at the elbow and steered him toward the elevator. In handcuffs.

"Dekker." Toby reached them before they cleared the last row of cubicles.

Ivan lunged at him but came up short and glared at Dekker. "Don't think this is over, Hendricks. I'll get even with you, just like I will Blackmon." He snarled, his gold tooth shining.

"Easy there. Those cuffs can get uncomfortable if you move around too much," Dekker said.

"Oh, please tell me what the charges are. I want to make sure I get it right for the article." Toby welcomed the buzzing zip driving the blood faster through his veins. It might be petty to enjoy the sight of the other man's downfall, but Ivan had been more than willing to sacrifice Toby to the law in his quest for revenge. It was nice to see he was being held accountable for his actions.

"You won't be writing anything. I'll see to that," Ivan snapped.

Dekker and Toby looked at each other, both shaking their heads at the enraged man's futile ranting. Dekker dropped his hand to Ivan's wrist and he yelped. "I warned you that they would tighten up if you moved your hands around too much. Now, keep quiet while I finish my interview with Hendricks. We want to make sure we have all the facts straight for the story. No one wants to have to print a correction due to erroneous information."

It took all Toby had not to offer Dekker a high five. "What are you going to do with him?"

"Mr. Strong and I are going to take a little drive. Depending on what we find at his home with the search warrant that was just executed, we may add more charges to the ones I stated when I read him his rights. Illegal use of intellectual property, attempted theft of classified information from a government official, and there are some old charges of assault on a minor that may apply after we check the statute of limitations.

"He's going to be busy for a while with court dates. I don't think the prosecutor is comfortable having someone like him loose on the streets. He may be remanded until his actual trial begins sometime late next year."

"That's great. It couldn't happen to a more deserving person." Toby was writing as fast as he could on the small notepad he'd pulled from his back pocket.

"Oh, and Toby." Dekker moved Ivan into the elevator, then kept his finger on the button to hold the doors open. "Don't leave town. The senator has something to discuss with you tomorrow."

He gave Ivan a cold glare. "*He* fired me. I've already applied for a job in Atlanta."

"Don't. Not yet. Wait until you speak to the senator."

"But—" The doors closed in front of him.

Well, nothing for Atlanta had been finalized yet. He pulled out his phone. A quick text message had his move to Atlanta on hold until the senator was through with him. And if Ivan was gone, was he still fired? Maybe Senator Blackmon had a lead on a new job for him. *Not likely.*

He packed up all his personal items from his cubicle but left the box under his desk. He'd hear what Senator Blackmon had to say tomorrow, then he'd figure out what to do with the box and his career. He'd packed his nameplate, a photo of him and Pops at a Braves game, a stress ball—a requirement for anyone with Ivan as their boss—and the journalism awards he'd won since he began his career as a reporter ten years ago. Where had the time gone?

By now, he should be higher up the totem pole and not because of some plan. But the managing editor retired right after the paper had been sold a few years back. The new owners weren't local. And Ivan's credentials had sounded impressive, even to him. So Ivan got the job.

Toby turned his computer on and began typing up the story on Ivan's arrest. He'd leave out the assault charge for now. Both Senator Blackmon and Abby would have to give him permission to use their names in relation to the charges. Maybe he should find it strange that after being the outsider among this group of Gina's influential friends that suddenly a spot had cleared for him, but he didn't. He was following the course before him, trusting God to lead the way.

He'd spent so much time around them with Gina it was almost as if he was one of them. But without her, the sense of warmth, the kinship and camaraderie were missing. The senator and Jeremy would continue to speak to him and when they encountered one another, they would interact in a manner that went deeper than just social acquaintances. Yet without Gina, without the glue that bonded the group together, there would be a weakest link. One that had been twisted and pulled on until the connection wasn't as true as the others were. He was that link. And he always would be without her there making him stronger.

Gina spent her lunch hour exchanging gifts she'd bought her nieces and nephews for Christmas that weren't the right size. Which was frustrating considering she'd checked with their parents about sizing not a month earlier. Growth spurts were the bane of her holiday shopping list.

She hurried into the office, unsure if Abby had returned from lunch with a client. Jeremy was in the waiting area, thumbing through a magazine.

When she walked in, he looked up and smiled. "I hope you don't mind, I felt foolish waiting in my car when I have a key."

He could not be embarrassed or making excuses for letting himself into his wife's office. Or was he? "No problem. I'm sorry I was late getting back and you had to sit here waiting. Abby had a client lunch, but I'm sure she won't be much longer."

"That's fine. I'm not here to see her. I came to see you."

"Oh. Okay. Well, um, what can I do for you?"

He dropped his gaze to his shoes. His awkwardness didn't bode well. She hadn't done anything to cause a problem while working on the recreation center project. With a forced laugh, she watched his face for signs of…something.

"Have you seen Toby Hendricks in the last couple of days?"

His question caught her so off guard, she sat down on the edge of the chair closest to her. "No, not since the day his article about the senator ran in the paper."

"That's what I thought. Do you believe he spent time with you, posing as your friend, just so he could get information?"

"He admitted that's what his boss told him to do. So, yes, I do believe he was using me for the chance to be close to all of you."

"We all thought of Toby as a hanger-on. And I'll admit I was never comfortable having him around before..." His voice faded and he shrugged.

"Before you married Abby?" Gina couldn't help the question in her voice.

He stood up. "If I tell you something in confidence, will you give me your word that you won't discuss it with anyone, including Abby?"

She did love to know the inside details of everything. She just never imagined her minister would be the one filling in those details. "Okay, but I hope this is something Abby knows because if she ever found out you told me and not her, I won't be responsible for what she does to you."

"Abby knows. Her father is who freed me of my camera shyness 'issue.'"

"Oh." Because really, what else could she say?

"Let's go into your office, if you don't mind."

She led the way down the short hall and motioned Jeremy to a chair. She closed the door and took her place behind her desk. "I promise I won't reveal what you tell me nor will I discuss it or ask you questions about it after we finish this conversation."

He nodded and offered her a warm smile. "Thank you. I can't give you all the specifics regarding my situation because, well, it isn't allowed. But I can share enough to hopefully help you see where I'm coming from."

She resisted the urge to growl. No telling how much trouble she'd be in. He was her minister, after all, but if he didn't just spit it out, she was going to die of unsatisfied curiosity. "What are you trying to tell me?"

Jeremy met her gaze and nodded as if he knew his rambling was driving her crazy. "The reason I was so uncomfortable around Toby was his profession. I had spent my entire adult life avoiding any type of media attention. Once my parents were gone, that wasn't as necessary. Are you with me so far?"

Gina folded her arms in front of her on the desk and leaned forward. "You're still being mysterious, but what I think you're saying is that the reason you didn't do interviews or allow yourself to be photographed was because your parents were alive. Is that it?"

He smiled. "Yes, exactly. And that's what you can't tell anyone. Especially not Toby."

She rolled her eyes. "Pastor, I won't be telling Toby anything because I won't be seeing him."

"Maybe. But still, I will hold you to your word about my secret."

"We're solid. I would never betray your trust in me."

"Thank you. Now getting back to Toby." He quirked a brow at her heavy sigh.

"Sorry, it's just that you're the last person I would expect to try and advocate for him considering your aversion to all things media related."

"I know. And maybe that's why God chose me to be the one to talk to you. I'm probably the only person who could ask you to try to understand the position Toby's boss put him in. I've always avoided him, not willing to answer his questions, but he still had to write articles that involved me. None of us have made his job easy, yet he's always printed the truth about the incidents he was covering. He never held our lack of cooperation against us on the page. He'd have to have a pretty tough skin to hang around people he knew weren't comfortable having him around and not try to get a dig in here or there, don't you think?"

"Yes, he would. And Toby does. He also has a thick head. He and I have joked about his quest for the story of all stories. About how he would do anything to get that story. He preyed on my friendships with Katherine and Abby and through them, you, Nick and the senator. Even Judge Pierce. He used to tease me about my faith. That more than anything is what kept me safe from falling for his charm."

"Do you believe it's possible for a man to change?"

"Of course, but only if he wants to change. Toby never saw anything wrong with what he was doing. He told me the main reason he didn't steal the prayer journal was because he was afraid of being caught and embarrassing his grandfather."

"He wasn't raised in church like you and I were. But when he was a boy, his grandparents took him to church with them. That's more than a lot of people experience. And even though he was noticeably uncomfortable at our wedding reception, when he was in trouble so deep and so dark he couldn't find his way out, he came to church looking for help."

Gina fought the prickles around her heart. She wasn't the one who was wrong. "Jeremy, I appreciate your concern and what you're trying to do. I've spent a lot of time with Toby. I know about his goals and his plans. He won't date the same woman more than twice because she might get the crazy idea he's interested in her."

He sat back and stretched out in his chair with a cocky smirk on his face. Not an expression she was used to seeing on him unless he and Nick were giving each other a hard time.

"How many times have you gone on a date with Toby?"

"Never."

"Excuse me? I thought the definition of a date was two people going to dinner, a movie, a party or some other outing."

"Yes, that's a date. But Toby only came to those things with me when I didn't have a real date. He took me to the movies whenever it was his week to write the movie-review column and the new release was a chick flick. He falls asleep trying to watch one. He expenses my ticket, the box of popcorn and the soda he buys me in exchange for an explanation of the heroine's motives in the movie." She jabbed her finger against the stack of papers on her desk. "If the guy expenses your snacks, it isn't a date."

"Did you enjoy spending time with him?"

"What?" She closed her eyes and shook her head, willing her eyes not to betray her. "Why are you doing this?"

"I don't know. I just know that last Sunday when I looked out on the congregation, he was up in the balcony with five seats open all around him and he looked lost. Not from God. We've had some deeply spiritual discussions and I've answered some questions he didn't want to ask his grandfather."

"His grandfather?" She scooted to the edge of her seat. "You know his grandfather?"

"Yes, don't you?"

"No, I don't. And that should tell you something right there. He talks about him all the time. He loves his grandfather. That's probably his one redeeming quality in my eyes considering how much I love Gigi. But I've never met him."

"Has he met Gigi?"

"No. I told you, we don't have that type of relationship."

"But you admit you do have a relationship."

"Fine. Yes, on my side, I thought he was my friend. I was even starting to notice more about him than his annoying attitude. But the only reason he tried to get to know me was as a means to an end. I was his friend. He wasn't mine."

"Why don't you have a steady boyfriend?"

"I'm sorry, Jeremy, but I have no idea why my dating status would matter to you at all."

"Gina, you're very good friends with my wife and Katherine. And I'd like to think that we're friends. And I'm your pastor, as well. Can't I be concerned about you?"

"The pastor card, really?" She blew out a frustrated breath. "Fine, I'll explain. God has the perfect mate picked out for me. He knows who it is. And He will send him my way when He's ready. Hanging out with Toby while I was waiting helped pass the time. Nothing more."

"So you don't love him?"

Her heart froze. Actually all of her froze. She couldn't breathe. Worse, she wasn't sure she could say no. Not if she didn't want to lie to her pastor.

Oh, no. What had her heart done to the rest of her?

She was going to be sick. She jumped up from her desk and ran from the room. In the bathroom, she leaned against the tile wall, letting its coolness soothe her until her breathing calmed. The nausea faded, but Jeremy's question wouldn't stop clanging around in her head. How could she love the man who had used her to get ahead in his career?

She was smarter than that. She'd told herself he was safe because she knew he had an agenda and that she and romance were not part of his plan.

She bumped her head against the wall, hoping to knock some sense into herself. This realization didn't change anything. Even if she had fallen for him, she didn't have to stay down, wallowing in the misery of crazy love. Because that's what this was—crazy.

She would not let herself love Toby Hendricks. God couldn't think he was the perfect mate for her. Because her soul mate wouldn't be a man who looked as if he'd never touched a razor, who tried to advance his career on the backs of her friends and who never had a kind word to say to her. All Toby ever did was criticize and provoke her. He didn't even like her.

As she berated herself and ticked off countless reasons why her heart should not be beating a fast *thu-thump*, her forehead and her fingers tingled with the warm tenderness of those two stupid and completely non-Toby kisses he'd laid on her the night she was terrified of what she'd find at the hospital.

Suddenly her memory of his face wasn't an image of him sporting a cocky smirk. It was of a strong jaw-line and lips without jokes or unkind words passing across them. He'd held her hand when she'd been the most frightened in her life. And he hadn't teased her. He'd consoled her. Comforted her.

She wanted to slide down into a heap of whimpering denial, but the truth was as clear as the image of his piercing blue eyes when he'd settled them on her in the ER. A truth that had been there in front of her for longer than she would admit. She fought with him because she liked the fighting. No matter how bad her day had been, if he popped by the office or it was movie-review night, a few minutes scrapping and sniping with him made her forget she was tired or frustrated about something else.

But loving Toby didn't change the fact that he hated the town she never wanted to leave. So much so, he was willing to use her to gain access to the senator's home and steal information. The cold shock of her newly discovered feelings shifted to the chill of lonely despair. Neither she nor Pemberly were part of Toby's big plans for his future. She couldn't—no, she wouldn't try to change his mind. Because as ungodly as it was to have it, she wasn't letting go of her pride. It held her mind steady, stopping her heart from being swayed. Keeping it safe from more heartbreak.

Chapter 10

"What is this mess?" Pops spat the half-chewed cookie into a napkin and glared at Toby.

"It's a sandwich cookie." Toby met his displeased glare with steady determination. "With less sugar." He held up the package for proof.

"Why less sugar? What's wrong with the real thing? Were they out? If so, the grocery store you passed on your way in has a whole section dedicated to them. They even have the ones with twice the filling that you keep forgetting to buy."

"I'm not the one forgetting you have diabetes. Eat your cookie and enjoy it or I'll bring you celery sticks next time."

"You do and I'll take my cane to you." He grumbled but he dunked the cookie in his cup of milk for the seven-count, then popped it into his mouth. He flinched as he swallowed. "It's not the same."

"I know, but a good friend's grandmother was just rushed to the hospital recently because she'd had too much sugar. I don't want to have you go through that."

"I check my sugar every day. It's been right where the doctor said he wants it. He knows about the sandwich cookies." He dropped his eyes to the floor. "I told him when my three-month A1C test showed my levels were higher than usual. But he said it was fine for me to indulge my sweet tooth as long as it was only once a week. And now here you are, trying to deny an old man his one guilty pleasure. It pains my heart to know you can be that cold toward your grandfather."

Toby's swallow of milk went down wrong and he beat his chest with the side of his fist. "Pops," he wheezed. "You can try that guilt trip on a candy striper, but don't expect it to work on me. I talked to the doctor, too."

"That's invading my privacy. Just because you're some uppity reporter in tight with a senator and a city councilman doesn't give you the right to go behind my back with my own doctor."

"Are you done with the righteous outrage? That was one of your better efforts." But he wasn't letting Pops guilt-trip him about something as serious as ruining his health. He loved him too much to let him even think he could. He cocked a smirk at the indignant man. "Or is your memory going and you've forgotten that mountain of paperwork you insisted I sign, making me responsible for your ornery self?"

"You'd like that, wouldn't you? When I get too frail and you have to put forth some effort to look after me, you'll pack up my apartment and ship me across the lake to the nursing home. I won't get any more cookies and you won't have to waste your time coming to see me. You'll have the nurses email you a progress report once a week, no, once a month because you can't be bothered with an old coot like me. Well, in the meantime, I might just change my will and you won't get anything."

Toby stared, a rushing burn surging forth from somewhere near his stomach, up through his chest until it seared the back of his throat. His grandfather firmed his jaw and glowered at him in defiance.

He stood up and took the two steps necessary to tower over his grandfather. Leaning down, he gripped the arms of the chair, caging him in and bringing them almost nose to nose. Whether Pops was kidding or he really thought Toby came to see him for that reason, he didn't know, but he was going to banish it from Pops's mind this second. "Listen to me, old man, and listen well because we're not going to have this conversation again. I am not my father. I don't think my life would be easier if you were gone. It would be emptier.

"I've stayed in this town, kept working for a man I didn't like or even respect because it kept me near you. I come visit you because I *want* to see you. If I wanted to get rid of you, I'd take the coward's way out, call Dad and turn you over to him. I signed the papers giving me access to your health and financial information because I needed to make sure you were being taken care of, not just for you, but also for me. I love you.

"I don't want to see you disrespected and thrown aside again like Mom and Dad did when we moved in with you. They should have let you live with us instead of banishing you to this place." A sweeping motion of his arm encompassed the room around them. "The whole reason they moved to Pemberly was to take care of you after your stroke."

Toby pushed himself up and away, reclaiming his seat. His grandfather's eyes glistened with a watery sheen, turning them almost clear instead of the light blue color Toby had inherited from him.

He smiled. He'd inherited most of his good traits from this man. And Pops thought he was a burden. Far from it. He was Toby's ballast, keeping him level when he began to list to one side, just like Gina did. He hissed out a harsh breath at that truth. "I hope that's the last of the crazy talk or I'll be putting a call in to Dr. Jacobs to see about getting you a psych evaluation. Is that clear?"

Pops pulled his handkerchief out of his back pocket and wiped his eyes. He nodded his head, keeping his gaze downcast. "Your father never told you why y'all moved here, did he?"

"They moved here to take care of you after you had the stroke." Toby watched a somber grimace take possession of Pops's face. The embers of the fire that had just died down in his stomach flared. "Didn't they?"

"Not exactly."

"What do you mean 'not exactly'?"

"I promised Jeffrey I wouldn't tell you. And he promised he would. It looks like he's as reliable in this as he is in everything else for his family."

"Pops, just say it."

"Yes, I'd had a stroke, but it was a very minor one. I regained full use of my arms and legs and my fingers before I completed my prescribed physical therapy here." He looked around his apartment, tapping his thumb against his cane, lost in the past. "I was over at the nursing home, but because I was improving so quickly they had a vacant apartment and asked me if I wanted to stay here for the rest of the allotted time as a test to see how I would do at home when they released me."

Toby watched him, leaning forward to hear every word and praying for God to give Pops the strength and comfort to say what was on his heart.

He cleared his throat and shifted in his chair. "I called your father to let him know how much better I was doing and that it looked like I was going to be able to take care of myself. I expected him to be relieved, but he got angry and started yelling.

"Turns out his company was downsizing. His department and his high salary were the first ones they got rid of. He had taken a second and third mortgage out on their house and he was already starting to fall behind on the house payments and the high-interest credit cards he had maxed out."

"Wait a minute." Toby held his hand up to stop his grandfather. "I thought Dad was one of the main vice presidents in the company. He took an early retirement to come here."

Pops was shaking his head. "No, he was a bean counter in a middle-management position that could have been done at half the expense by one of the more experienced accounting clerks. He's always been a bigger success in his mind than his paycheck supported. He never wanted your mother to work even though she'd earned a better degree than him."

The air conditioner cycled on and the cool air blew

down on Toby's head. His father had lied to him, had been lying to him for years. "But why did you come live here? We could have stayed with you until he found another job and got back on better financial footing."

Pops shook his head back and forth. "Your father had already filed for bankruptcy. He was going to salvage what he could, but he was counting on living in my house. He'd surrendered y'all's in the bankruptcy. His attorney wasn't able to convince the trustee that he couldn't pay back part of the monies he owed so his debts weren't discharged. They put him and your mother on a restructured payment plan. It took him three years to pay back a quarter of what they owed. And that was after I got him the job he has now that actually pays more than his old one."

"I still don't understand."

"Your father told me it was my fault he was put in that position. That I'd shamed him. If I'd died, he would have inherited the life insurance money and he could have paid off all their bills." Pops eyes were dry. His jaw was rigid and his voice turned to a low rumble. He looked sad. Not hurt, just very sad.

"I called Edward Delaney and had him draw up a trust for the house that allowed your parents to live there but blocked them from selling it without my approval. And upon my death, your approval. I had affidavits sworn out disclaiming your father's right to my life insurance policy and you named the sole beneficiary. That's why he treats you the way he does. And I'm sorry for it. I used to think it was my fault, but God showed me your father was blessed with the advantages I didn't have and instead of using them to help others with his excess, he kept it all and wasted it. That Scripture you referenced in your article about the senator—your father thinks that way. That he's above everyone else.

"He wished me dead. So I made myself dead to him. But I also ensured he'd always have a home by not putting the house in his or your mother's name. He doesn't see his mistakes, his weaknesses." Pops put his hand on Toby's knee. "Don't be like that. Admit when you're wrong and then try to do better. But always remember you're just like everybody else. How you use what you have says a lot about what's important to you."

Toby was numb inside. And it was best that way. He prayed God would give him strength to control the anger that would come when the numbness faded. "He said it would have helped him if you'd died? He really said that?"

Pops nodded. "*That* shames me. Money is worth more to your father than life. Grams and I didn't raise him that way. We did with him as we did with you when you visited. I never kept him from doing something he really wanted to do, but I did keep him from some things that I thought were a danger to his body or his soul. In college he joined a group he met on campus. After that, he changed. He started expecting more, telling me I owed him."

Toby stood up and walked over to stare out the living room window down at a corner of the English garden behind the solarium. He looked back over his shoulder. "What if I want the house? How do I get him out?"

"Don't do anything out of anger. Your outrage is

wasted on him, son. He doesn't think he's wrong. And when a man believes he's right, he'll fight you to the death. Our family is already torn apart enough."

"How much was the house worth when they moved in?" Toby didn't discount his grandfather's advice or his request. This wasn't about his father. Pemberly was his home and it would remain that way. It was where the two people he loved the most in the world lived. And he'd loved coming to his grandparents' home as a kid. In his teens, though, after he moved with his parents into the house, it hadn't felt the same. And now he knew why. Love had left that address with Pops's move to Sunny Days. Well, it was time it was restored to the happy, loving *home*, not house, it had been. And he couldn't think of anyone he'd rather make a home with than the very stubborn but dear to his heart Gina Lawson.

"Why are you smiling?" Pops was watching him.

"Sorry, I was envisioning someone standing in the kitchen threatening me with a wooden spoon." He grinned.

"Boy, watch out. You don't want a woman who can beat you at arm wrestling. Or checkers." He said in a lower voice.

Toby laughed. "If Gina Lawson thinks I'm a temporary kind of guy, she's about the get the reality check of her life."

"Gina Lawson? Genevieve's granddaughter?"

Toby's heart did a double beat. "The woman you and Mrs. Montego have been trying to introduce me to is Gina Lawson? Shoulder-length, curly hair and a very sassy everything else?"

"Yes, she is the sweetest girl. Oh, how I've prayed God would soften your heart toward meeting her."

"If my heart was any softer toward her it would be marshmallow fluff. I want her as my wife and I want your house. We'll make it a home again."

He wrapped an arm around his grandfather and held him while they both wept for the unhappiness they'd endured from someone they had loved. "It'll be one of those skipped-generation things. The love in that house skipped over my parents, but I inherited it from you." Toby wiped his eyes. "Now, I have to go see a lawyer about a house and convince a woman who doesn't like me to marry me so I can spend the rest of my life arguing with her."

Pops followed him to the door. "If there's anything Genevieve and I can do to help you win your sweetheart, let us know. We've prayed for so long that you two would find each other."

"Oh, we found each other. It's figuring out what to do with what we've found that's the tricky part. But I have a few ideas."

Abby and Katherine pounced on Gina as soon as the maître d' delivered her to their booth at Cristo's. It was the one in the back corner, next to the emergency exit. No traffic. No witnesses. Gina slid into her seat facing both attorneys and realized the setting was eerily similar to an interrogation scene she'd watched on a late-night television cop show. Well, they could have at her. She hadn't done anything wrong.

Katherine's steady gaze didn't waver until they'd placed their drink and meal orders. "What is going on with you?"

"I have no idea what you're talking about." It was the equivalent of pleading the Fifth Amendment.

Tag. Abby came out scolding. "Don't try that wide-eyed innocent look on me. What happened with Toby? And you don't get to say 'nothing' because I'm the one who told you." Her gaze dropped to the lacquered tabletop and she moved her glass in small loops in front of her. "I shouldn't have said what I did. I'm sorry."

"You don't think I had a right to know that he—" Gina sucked in a breath and gritted her teeth. She'd had enough of lying awake over half the night fighting an incessant urge to cry for no reason other than there wasn't anyone to fight with anymore. Of all the stupid, ridiculously insane reasons to be upset.

"What is going on?" Katherine asked.

Well if they wanted to know then fine, here it went. "What does it say about me that I'm at my happiest when I'm plotting or carrying out a planned skirmish with a cynical, yet attractively scruffy newspaper-man with eyes the light blue of a crisp winter day? It's not normal. Romance. Flowers like Nick gave you—and the puppy dog. Well, silk flowers because of my allergies."

Gina flung a hand toward Abby. "Or your prince locking the two of you in a room so you can't escape until he'd declared his undying love for you." She sniffed, trying to hold the tears back. "I want romance. I want to feel loved and special. And I deserve it. I want someone to do that for me so my heart can go pitter-patter. It's my turn."

Katherine scooted out of her side of the booth, came over to Gina's, and put her arms around her.

"You miss him, don't you? It's only natural. You spent a lot of time with him. But the right guy is out there for you. One who will do all those romantic things just for you. No woman deserves to be swept off her feet, or have her marriage proposal written in the clouds by a skywriter, more than you. And it will happen. You'll find him now that Toby's out of the way."

Gina cried into the jacket of Katherine's suit while Abby kept her hand supplied with fresh tissues. "I did find him."

Katherine pushed her back to look at her. "Where? Who?"

Gina's face crumpled and fat, hot tears seared trails down her cheeks. "It's Toby and it's awful. Both of you got a real prince. And I got the grumpy one who doesn't have a romantic bone in his body. On top of that, he's leaving. His boss fired him and he's going to leave."

Abby grabbed Gina's hands. "Wait. Are you saying that you're in love with Toby? Hendricks? Oh, why couldn't you have fallen for anyone else? This is going to cost me three basketball-shooting lessons."

Gina turned her head toward Abby. "What are you talking about?"

"Jeremy and I have been having a difference of opinion in regard to you and Toby. He's convinced you two love each other and I told him you can't stand Toby. All the two of you do is fight."

Katherine shook her head. "Nick and I fought like, well, cats and dogs, in family court. That's why Uncle Charles made us spend the weekend with him."

"But Katherine," Abby said. "She's threatened bodily harm to him, in front of witnesses, almost every time they're near each other. And he's never done anything nice for her. He's always baiting her, trying to make her lose her temper."

"Speak up anytime here, Gina. Abby and I shouldn't be the ones arguing the state of your relationship with Toby."

"There is no state. We don't have a relationship. I told him to go away."

"Then we'll find you someone else to fight with."

Gina glared at Abby. "Did we do this to you when you were so pathetic over Jeremy? No, we fed you chocolate and went for a spa day. You're acting as if finding me a man is as easy as taking an ad out in the newspaper for men meeting certain requirements. Well, Toby is the exception to the rule. On the surface, he is far away from the ideal guy for me. He's grouchy. The only person besides himself he cares about is his grandfather."

"Yes, Jeremy was telling me what a nice man his grandfather is."

"Of course he was. Everyone's met his grandfather except me."

"Gina, you need to decide whether you're mad at Toby or you miss him. You can't take action if you don't have a direction."

"Thanks, Katherine. Would taking action involve having your assistant create a biography out of news clippings of your archrival? Because that was what you had me do before you realized you loved him."

The waitress appeared with a heavy tray loaded down with their lunches. She placed a bowl of baked potato soup in front of each of them and a grilled cheese sandwich beside Katherine's soup and a chicken club for Abby. In front of Gina, she presented a huge stemmed goblet filled with vanilla ice cream liberally sprinkled with chunks of fudge brownie and drizzled with caramel and chocolate sauce with a swirl of whipped cream and a big cherry on top to complete the Broken Hearts featured staple.

Gina grinned and thanked the waitress, then turned back to her lunch partners. "Thank you. I don't feel as pathetic as I did."

"Really? I had no idea chocolate had such a restorative effect on the brokenhearted." Then, all kidding aside, Abby put her spoon down. "Anyone who hasn't been around me in the past few years still hasn't been able to get their chin off the floor when I tell them my husband is the minister of our church. It doesn't always matter what vocation they're in. They may be allergic to chocolate, which would be very sad, or be short, tall, grumpy, cynical, or scruffy. Love comes in all shapes and sizes so that there's one for each of us. It isn't a one size fits all. When you meet the perfect match for you, no one else compares. And only you know when that's who they are. You just feel it inside."

"Even if all we do is fight?"

Katherine cocked her head to the side. "He's never done anything nice for you?"

Gina's cheeks burned. "At the senator's birthday party, I was so terrified that Gigi was worse than my mom was letting on. Toby held my hand all the way to the hospital. He didn't let go until he'd pulled up to the door to let me out while he found a parking space. And after we knew she was going to be okay, he still offered to stay with me. I thought he wanted to leave and he got all huffy saying he wasn't trying to get rid of me, he just wanted me to know he was there for me." She looked up and Abby and Katherine were wearing identical, wide-eyed, mouth-open expressions. "What?"

"Oh, my. He does love you."

"What? No, he was just being kind because he loves Pops as much as I love Gigi. He could relate to the panic I was experiencing until I knew she was going to be fine.

"I realized I love him, but I also realized it would never work. The teasing banter is fun because we aren't around each other all the time. But when I get married, I want it to be to someone mature and even-tempered. I want to truly settle down. With Toby, there would be constant bickering and trying to best each other. That would get old really fast. It's better that he's leaving. I'll find that calm, reliable man God has lined up for me and all will be well."

Katherine handed Gina a spoon. "Eat your ice cream. It will help mask the taste of those fanciful words you don't believe for a minute."

Chapter 11

Toby turned toward Nick on the sidewalk. "I really appreciate your putting the proposal together for me and getting the paperwork filed so quickly. This helps my timeline a lot."

Nick shook the hand Toby offered him. "It's fine. I know a little bit about dealing with a manipulative parent. My dad cost me several years of happiness with Kat that I might have had if he hadn't interfered. Be strong. Look him in the eye and point out the benefits to him, but with the silent understanding that this is a courtesy visit not a requirement. If he knows what he's getting, he'll sign and you can have them out by next weekend."

"He's a yeller. He thinks I have a problem with authority."

Nick shot him a raised eyebrow. "No?"

Toby shrugged. "It depends on the authority figure."

He pressed his finger to the doorbell. A tinkling chime echoed through the house. His mother answered the door.

"Toby? We weren't expecting you. Is something wrong with your grandfather?"

He shook his head. "No, he's fine. I need to speak to you and Dad. It's business."

She cast an assessing glance at Nick, who offered her a brief nod. They followed her into the chilly house. The giant Oriental rug in the entryway should have been pretty but somehow managed to clash with the honeyed pine baseboards and the neutral tan walls. This room reflected his parents and their mercurial temperaments. Either too much or nothing, the gaudiness of excess forced into close proximity with the plain. He would donate whatever wasn't nailed down to charity and spend weekends with Gina antiquing until they filled the rooms with beautiful pieces of furniture that had an aged but loved look to them.

Gina. He was getting ahead of himself. His five-year plan might have been a bit arrogant since he'd neglected to include God in the planning. But he hadn't forgotten to seek God's guidance and wisdom in how to proceed with the biggest plan of his life.

First, he needed a house. And that's what this one was right now. After he sent his parents and their really bad furnishings packing, he'd put the next step into motion. Love. His summers spent here as a little boy had etched the warmth and the love between Pops and Grams into his memories, showing him how a home was different from a house.

As he followed his mother down the short hallway to the family room, he finally understood why a place he'd been so happy to visit for a few weeks every summer while his parents stayed away had felt cold to him when his parents and he moved into the house after Pops' stroke. His parents had stripped away every ounce of warmth and welcome his grandparents had spent their lifetimes pouring into this structure. He wanted to make it a real home, restore it to its old glory as a tribute to his grandparents.

His father was seated on the overly ornate sofa, reading the newspaper. It wasn't the *Sentinel*. He'd always thought the local paper a bit too "lowbrow" for his tastes. He had interests in much bigger and more important cities. No article found in the *Sentinel* would be as well-written or as informative as one from New York. On weekends, he did manage to read an Atlanta-based paper. He considered it adequate for supplying him with any "local" news.

"Hello, Dad." Toby's greeting didn't earn him even a twitch of the hand holding the paper up and out at arm's length. Not until his father finished reading whatever article he was looking at. He was either a very slow reader or thought to provoke Toby's impatience. Normally, it would work, but not today. Today, he would be the one doing the provoking.

The paper lowered, revealing a man with droopy jowls, a paunchy middle and a very receding hairline. His blue eyes had faded to a dull gray. They lacked the spark of mischief—happiness—that brightened Pops' eyes. And where Pops had laugh lines that crinkled at the corners of his eyes, his dad had deep lines carved into his forehead from years of frowning down on others.

"Is he dead?"

Toby's anger ignited, flaring high like dry kindling meeting a spark. He took a step toward his father when a firm hand caught his upper arm. He turned. Nick's look of caution reminded him why he was here. He shook his head to clear the red haze, then nodded and carefully modulated his voice. "No, he was doing just fine when I saw him yesterday. But you'd know that if you bothered to visit or call him."

"How or if I speak with my father is none of your business." His dad folded his paper in very precise halves then quarters before laying it aside, clearly communicating his displeasure at being interrupted before he was done. He cut his eyes toward Nick.

"Let me introduce my..." Toby hesitated over how to identify Nick.

But Nick stepped into the breach. "Nick Delaney, a friend of Toby's."

"Delaney? Any relation to that Edward Delaney who stole my inheritance from me?"

Toby had wondered how they would steer the conversation toward the legalities he was here to discuss, but he need not have worried. His father had opened the topic.

"Yes, he's my father," Nick said evenly.

"Then I want you out of my house." His father stood and jabbed his finger toward the doorway.

"Actually, Nick will be staying. We both will. You and I have some business to transact and he's my attorney."

He thought his father's face paled a shade or two, but then he drew a deep breath and any sign of weakness or concern was replaced by a sneer. "We have no joint business interests."

"No, we don't. And after today, I won't trouble you again." Toby motioned Nick to a wing chair at the other end of the coffee table and he took a seat on the sofa closest to Nick.

His father remained standing for a few moments before he straightened his shoulders and reclaimed his own seat as if he was still in control of the situation. "What do you want?"

His mother waited until his dad sat down, then took the chair at the opposite end of the coffee table, facing Nick. She threw Toby a frigid glare. She was as cold as his father was, but what it took his father a paragraph to say, his mother could convey with one icy stare.

"I'm well, and you?" He was baiting them, but he couldn't help himself.

His father turned a steely glare on him. "Sarcasm is the behavior of a child. A man in his thirties shouldn't stoop to such juvenile tactics to gain attention."

"I apologize for my childishness. I forgot you two have no sense of humor." He smiled, which caused a muscle to jump in his father's cheek.

Nick cleared his throat, then handed Toby a folder. Toby laid it on the coffee table between his father and himself.

"I'll be direct so we can be done and out of your way sooner. So you can get back to more important things." Toby angled his body toward his father. "I want the house."

"You can't have it."

"I can and you're going to give it to me."

"It isn't mine to give. But since you brought an attorney with you—a Delaney—you already know that."

"True. I also know that I'm Pops' sole heir and you two receive the use of this house for the remainder of your lives. It has no monetary value to you because you can't sell it or mortgage it to the hilt the way you did my childhood home."

"I am your father, and you don't have a right to question the choices I made on behalf of our family. They were mine to make."

"That was true in the past anyway. I'm here today to make you an offer. It's the only one you'll receive. If you refuse, it will cost you a lot of money."

"Are you planning to sue me?"

"No. Evict you."

"What!" His father was on his feet, glaring down at him.

His mother opened her mouth to spout something venomous, no doubt, but clamped her lips shut before striking.

Nick shifted in his chair. When Toby spared a glance in his direction, he wasn't sure, but he thought Nick was fighting not to laugh. His shoulders were shaking. Maybe their fathers' temperaments were similar after all.

"I'm willing to pay you the market value of this house at the time you moved in plus moving and storage expenses *if*, before we leave today, you sign this agreement to vacate the premises within ten days."

"Absolutely not." His father's indignant tone was coupled with a red flush that spread across his cheeks down his neck and beyond his shirt collar. He sat down.

"You will." Toby slid a piece of paper across the smooth surface of the coffee table. "Your current employer isn't doing well in this economy. The finance reporter at the *Sentinel* got the scoop on their plans to downsize."

"My job is secure."

"Is it as secure as the one you had in Tennessee?"

His father turned on him, fury firing the faded blue of his eyes to blue flame. "You have no idea what you're talking about. I weighed my options, and moving here was the best thing for me and for my family. Although my father couldn't stand to live under the same roof and chose to move into that retirement village."

"Pops told me about the layoff, the bankruptcy and the reason for the move here. And the house and the life insurance policy."

His father's jaw tensed and he straightened the cuff on his long-sleeved shirt before looking at Toby. "Your grandfather feels the need to control me. I explained to him that I was fully capable of providing for my family without his help. He just wanted to make sure the house stayed in the family. If he'd asked me not to sell it, he could have saved himself a lot of money in attorney's fees." His gaze flickered toward Nick.

"Toby, you shame your family by coming in here and disrespecting us like this." His mother tugged on the hem of her blouse while her eyes shot daggers at him and Nick.

Toby ignored her. "Dad, I'm offering you a decent amount of money. Today only. You're at an age and have been with the company long enough that early retirement won't change your benefits package much. This would be a chance for you and Mom to be free to do whatever you want. Travel, keep working, or buy a vacation home in the mountains or in Florida." He slid the paper toward his father. "Take the offer."

"And if I don't? Would you really evict your parents? Do you want the whole town of Pemberly to know how mercenary you can be toward your own flesh and blood? You won't be able to look anyone in this town in the eye ever again if you do it. So don't come to me making threats you don't have the backbone to carry out."

Toby held his hand out to Nick, who popped his briefcase open and handed him a manila envelope. Toby, in turn, handed it to his father. "Consider yourself notified of my intention to evict you. It will take me twenty extra days to get you out of here, but you'll still be gone—and without any financial recompense."

His father tossed the envelope on the sofa near his paper and rose to his feet. "You won't."

Toby stood, keeping himself at eye level with his father. "I have the sworn affidavits from the witnesses from the tear you went on while Pops was at the rehab center after his stroke. The security guard who forcibly removed you. The nurse and the doctor who were in the hall and heard you scream, 'Why couldn't you just die so I could have the life insurance?'" He stepped into his father's space.

His father tried to step back, but the end table had him trapped. "Lies, it's all lies. I would never say that to my father."

"Apparently you would and at a much louder volume than some people use at a football game. Sign the paper, take the money you aren't really entitled to but I'm willing to pay to have you gone. Or I will evict you and the 'little local paper' will print the article I write about the sins of the father, and the son's retribution in the name of his elderly grandfather. The people of Pemberly might hear about you being evicted by your own son, but they'll also learn that it's been a long time coming. And a lot nicer than what you deserve."

Nick offered Toby's dad a pen and a smile.

Gina stopped at the local coffee shop on her way in to work. It had been two weeks since Katherine and Abby's intervention, as they liked to call it. She was still not getting enough sleep, lying awake half the night, wishing she could fight with Toby again.

He'd started a series of articles on love and marriage, and how men's and women's expectations differed. She was tempted to fire off a scathing letter to the editor ticking off his woeful lack of qualifications on either subject. But she'd deleted the document immediately after she typed it last night. Somehow just capturing her thoughts on the screen had been enough to get her over her outrage at Toby Hendricks, commitmentphobe extraordinaire, and the insane idea that he believed he was any kind of authority on love and marriage.

Oh, how she wanted to pick a fight with him. It was almost as if he were taunting her. But that was ridiculous. Toby Hendricks was just padding his résumé so that readership would be up when he left behind the *Sentinel*, Pemberly, his grandfather and her. It was enough to make her want to box his ears.

She was mentally reminding herself of all the reasons she wasn't speaking to him as she sorted the mail and then went into Katherine's office to leave it on her desk. The morning edition of the *Sentinel* was laid flat with the headline in clear view. "Hometown Reporter Does Good but Wants Better."

Of course he does. He's greedy. She hadn't read her copy yet. Katherine was out on visits and Gina was trying to collate all the paperwork requiring her signature so it could be taken care of all at once. But she could spare a few minutes. She sat down at Katherine's desk and picked up the newspaper.

Toby was the new managing editor—for the *Sentinel*. He wasn't leaving. This holiday season had opened his eyes to the flaws in his opinions about family, loyalty, honesty, love and marriage. He wasn't as progressive in his views as he'd thought he was. He was just a small-town, forever kind of guy.

When pigs fly! He was out of his mind. Well, so much for missing him and wishing for what wasn't. Thank goodness he wasn't hers. Because two adjectives she would never attach to his name were *small-town* and *forever*. Ooh, he was so infuriating.

Katherine came in and stopped short. "I know you're insanely efficient with managing Abby's and my offices, but don't start thinking you can practice law, too. At least not without those hours and hours of law school first."

Gina huffed out a harsh breath and rose to her feet. "No, I saw the headline of the paper when I brought the mail in and I wanted to read the article."

"And, what did it say?"

"Toby's staying. He took over his boss's job and he's a forever kind of guy." She slapped the newspaper down on the desk. "Did you know that leading up to Valentine's Day he's writing a series of articles on love and marriage? I mean, we're talking about a man who gets the hives if he has to write an article for the commitments section of the paper." She was pacing back and forth, waving her hands around as she talked and then whacked her pinkie against the desk. "Ow!"

"See, God doesn't like you getting all worked up over someone you said was the worst possible match for you."

"He is. I mean, all we do is fight. The only time he's ever been nice to me is when Gigi was in the hospital. Well, there was the time Shaun insulted Frannie."

"Shaun insulted Frannie? When?"

"At the reception. He came into the kitchen while I was helping out. He thought she couldn't be a good business manager if she didn't bring enough servers. I was about to tell him off and Toby came in. He kept me from saying something I would have regretted."

"It sounds to me like fighting isn't all you and Toby have in common. In fact, it may just be that you're attracted to each other but don't know what to do about it or are too scared to find out."

Gina snorted and shifted her stance until one hip was cocked to the side. "Oh, please. I'm not afraid of anything involving that man. And I'll admit, if he shaved and cut his hair, he might be attractive, but Toby Hendricks is not a man to change his habits or make sacrifices for a woman. He's as allergic to a razor as he is to commitments."

"You know him best. I defer to your wisdom on the subject."

Gina snatched up her paperwork and moved toward the door. "I have work to do and talking about Toby is a waste of time I can't spare."

Gina stayed busy for the rest of the day. Katherine had started taking more files home and dictating her case notes at night, then giving her the little tapes for transcription in the mornings. The new procedure was working well and offered Gina more flexibility in completing her tasks, like leaving a few minutes early and dropping the outgoing mail at the post office on her way home instead of making two trips.

She walked through the automatic doors and took her place in line behind a guy in a business suit. He glanced back at her and offered a big smile. She smiled back.

He looked at her again, then pulled out his newspaper and opened it. "Are you Gina Lawson from the paper?"

Huh? "I'm Gina, but I don't work for the paper."

"No, the pictures of you in the paper on the back page. Here, look for yourself." He handed her his copy, then walked to the next available window.

She set the certified envelopes in her hand on top of the display of shipping boxes and turned the wrinkled paper to the back page.

And screamed.

There on the entire, huge, every-inch-covered back page of the evening edition of the *Sentinel* was a collage of pictures of couples from different time periods. And every one had Toby's face for the man and hers for the woman.

One was clearly that shot from *Gone with the Wind* where Rhett carried Scarlett in his arms—of course with Toby's face on Rhett Butler's body and hers on

Scarlett's. Antony and Cleopatra. Sonny and Cher. She made a mental note to strangle him for that one. There was a snapshot of the *American Gothic* painting with their faces superimposed over the real ones. The two on the bottom were cutouts of her in her bridesmaid dresses at Katherine's and Abby's weddings. And worst of all, Toby's face was superimposed over Nick's and then Jeremy's.

The guy who had given her the paper stopped in front of her. "So, what's your answer?"

Still reeling with shock at seeing such kindergarten level cutting and pasting, she finally focused on the short article.

The new managing editor of the Sentinel *is happy with his new position but worries he'll get bored. His former position with this paper had him covering the political beat. And that's where he met his favorite verbal sparring partner, legal assistant Gina Lawson.*

Toby Hendricks claims he'll be able to do his new job more effectively if Ms. Lawson will grant him an interview. He needs to ask her something.

She shoved the paper back at the man. "I'm going to strangle him, that's my answer to this—this—poor use of the paper's ad space." She spun on her heel and marched toward the door.

"You forgot your mail." He rushed to bring her the handful of envelopes with the green return-receipt signature cards stuck to the back. He reached into his jacket pocket and pulled out a card. "If you turn him down, give me a call. I'll argue with you anytime."

Her face was on fire. Did all anyone think she was good for was picking fights? This was Toby's fault.

It was always Toby's fault. But this—this time he'd gone too far. When she got her hands on him, she was going to choke him.

"Thanks, but I only fight with him." She wasn't sure, but she thought he mumbled, "Lucky guy."

How she didn't run a red light on her way to the newspaper offices was beyond her. Maybe God understood just how riled she was. She was humiliated. He'd stuck her picture all over the back of the paper for all of Pemberly to see. And saying he was miserable because he didn't have anyone to argue with. With him as their boss, most of the staff at the paper would be growling at him within a week.

She pulled up to the curb and got out of her car, adding a little extra muscle to her efforts to slam the door. When she got closer to the glass doors of the *Sentinel* building, the guard hurried to open the door for her.

"Miss Lawson, it's good to see you." His smile was as big as a kid's was on Christmas morning.

"Thank you. Go ahead and call him. I'm sure he assigned you lookout duty." She motioned toward the phone on his desk. He nodded and hurried around it to pick up the receiver. Well, she knew what floor she needed. Pity it wasn't higher. She could just toss Toby out of his new office's window. She strode to the elevator and punched the button, stepped in and pushed the button for his floor.

When the elevator doors opened, the thorn in her side himself was propped against the desk facing the elevator. She stood straight and cinched the belt on her coat. He pushed away from the desk and came toward her with slow but determined strides. His gaze locked onto her. Something was different.

He'd gotten a haircut. She could see his ears. And his eyes. His intense, clear blue eyes. And his face. There was no disfiguring scar anywhere to be seen, just smooth, closely shaved skin. When he smiled at her, a dimple dug deep into his lower cheek. Who knew?

She stood just inside the elevator car trying to process the image of the man coming at her with a lazy, dimpled smile aimed directly at her. Her mouth went dry. He was in a navy blue suit, with a dress shirt the color of his eyes and a perfectly tied tie. There wasn't a crease or wrinkle to be found in any part of his outfit. He could model for a menswear ad.

Her knees wobbled the closer he came. He stopped just on the other side of the threshold. "Welcome to the *Sentinel*, Miss Lawson."

"Don't even think about trying to charm me after making me the laughingstock of Pemberly."

"What?"

"The full-page ad on the back of the paper, Toby. I saw what you did."

He stepped into the elevator. His proximity sent her a step back as she tried to maintain her personal space. She folded her arms in front of her, cupping her elbows with her hands. "How could you do it?"

"Let's wait until we get downstairs. I have something to—"

"Ask me. Yeah, I read it. The guy standing in front of me at the post office read it and asked me out."

He moved as if to come closer to her. "What? I hope you turned him down."

"You don't get to decide who I date."

"I will before we're through today."

"Of all the chauvinistic, Neanderthal statements to make. Obviously, you've already forgotten the meaning of politically correct. You may carry some clout around here, and you may have even cleaned yourself up so they'll take you seriously as their boss, but I know you, Toby Hendricks. You're going to look like a complete idiot if you print any of your ideas regarding love and marriage."

The elevator stopped at the lobby and the doors opened. Toby propelled her out and across the tiled floor toward the entrance to the building. The security guard held the door, giving her a wink as they passed by. This was getting more bizarre by the minute.

A blast of cold air hit her in the face, bringing her back to the reality of Toby escorting her out of the building. Fine, they could finish this discussion out in the freezing cold. She was wearing a coat and he wasn't.

He caught her hand in his and laced their fingers, using the connection to drag her along with him toward the cement bridge.

"What has gotten into you?"

He brushed a stray curl away from her face and smiled. "You."

"Oh, no you don't. I read that in your little article. You are not blaming this on me. I didn't do anything."

"No, you did it just by being you."

"Huh?"

"Look, there are only two people in this world who really matter to me. Pops and you."

"I'm sorry the number of people you value is so limited, but isn't that your fault, not ours? And how in the world are you going to pull off a series of articles about family, loyalty, honesty, love and marriage? I'm not helping you."

"You are the most infuriating woman," he said, his words at odds with the amusement in his voice.

She jammed her knuckles against her hips and stood facing him. Her eyebrow lifted in question.

"Don't you understand I'd do anything for either one of you?"

"Toby, I fully believe you'd do anything for your grandfather. Me? No, I don't believe that. I'm a game when you're bored or frustrated with your job and want to vent."

"Why can't you see me as a serious person? As a man with goals?"

"One of your goals was to steal from a US senator. You used me to create the opportunity. Now you've plastered my face all over the back of the evening edition of the paper in kindergarten cutouts. How do those actions help your case? You're just as reckless and self-absorbed as ever."

He gritted his teeth. He didn't look amused anymore. "You are…" He blew out a heated breath. "I wasn't going to steal it. Now can we talk about something else?"

Not giving in to his weak dodge, she kept pushing. "Senator Blackmon caught you in his study with the desk drawer open and the notebook in your hand."

"I wanted to see what was in it, okay? I was hoping it would have some secret I could use against Ivan to make him leave me alone." His gazed dropped to his shoes. "I was looking for the easy way out. I wouldn't have stolen it because it would have shamed Pops and I would have lost you."

"Saving the fact that you never 'had' me to lose for a later discussion, why did you even go into his private study? You could have approached the senator with at least part of Ivan's plan and given him the opportunity to help you or offer another means of thwarting Ivan."

"I thought I could resist the temptation."

"Right, because you are the epitome of self-control. All it took was sending you to the bathroom across the hall from the ultimate journalistic treasure and you forgot everything you held near and dear. Nice try, but I'm not buying it."

He growled, but she didn't flinch. "I thought that because I was with you I was safe from temptation."

Her eyes widened, then closed to mere slits. "Now it's my fault? Hendricks, how like you to pass the buck. Any convoluted logic that keeps your conscience clear so you can sleep at night. I have no sway over you. You do what you want, when you want and how you want. You wanted that notebook and you took it. When has there ever been anything you wanted that you didn't grab up in your hands before anyone else could touch it?"

"You're right." He tangled his fingers in the riot of curls at the side of her face, tilted her head to the ideal angle and kissed her. Hard. Pouring his frustration, fear and faith that they were meant to be together into his efforts. It was that or choke her. And she was kissing him back. She was the most infuriating, combative woman he'd ever met in his life. And as much as he wanted to throttle her, he wanted to hold on to her and never let her go.

Her lashes fluttered slowly apart. Her eyes were a bit glazed and her lips puffy. "What'd you do that for?" Her voice was a breathy, so-not-like-Gina whisper.

"I couldn't resist. You know how weak I am around temptation. And you tempt me."

Her reaction couldn't have been more opposite of what he was going for than if he'd thrown a glass of ice water in her face. "Now I'm a vice."

"Mercy, woman. I was paying you a *compliment*. A very big one, if I do say so myself. Which I believe I just did. Now, let's get down to the real reason I brought you out here."

He maneuvered her to a specific spot at the railing of the bridge, adding more effort to his tugging when she locked her knees in place instead of taking the few steps he wanted. He smoothed her hair where it was tousled. Then grabbing her hands, he held them to his lips before dazzling her with a huge smile. And dropped to his knee before her.

"What are you doing? Are you crazy?" Her gaze darted around like a cat chasing a dragonfly.

"Yes, Gina, I am. I'm crazy for you."

She reached down and tugged, trying to make him stand up. "No, you're not. Now stop this, please. Don't you dare use your knowledge of my weakness for romantic gestures to pull a prank on me. This isn't funny. Please get up."

He untangled her arms from around his and caught her at the elbows, holding her still. "Gina, when I stand up I'm going to kiss you again. And I'm going

to ask you the same question whether I'm on my feet
or my knees. I just wanted you to see that you're the
only woman with the power to bring me to my knees."

Oh, goodness, he was serious. Her head spun and
she swayed. He caught her. He always managed to
catch her. "This can't be happening. You have a five-
year plan, remember? One that doesn't include—this."

"I changed my mind. Actually, you changed my
heart."

"But we fight all the time. We can't be in a room
together for ten minutes without arguing."

He trilled his tongue, making a deep rumbly sound.

Her tummy flipped and her heart stuttered. This
wasn't possible. She reached out a hand and rested
it against his jaw. His clean-shaven jaw. She'd never
seen him without stubble and she still couldn't get
used to how handsome he was. "What did you do?"

He let his finger glide across her lips. "Shh, it's my
job to ask the questions. You provide the answers." He
straightened his position on his knees. "I should have
worn knee pads. I knew you wouldn't cooperate."

"I hardly—"

"Now, now, gorgeous, I didn't mean that the way
you're obviously taking it. I practiced this speech all
night, and you're going to hear me out."

She arched a saucy eyebrow because every part of
Gina Lawson exuded sass, but she remained silent.

"What I'm trying to say is, no, I didn't plan on
falling in love. No, I didn't plan to stay in Pemberly,
and no, I definitely didn't plan on my happiness depending on yours. But that doesn't stop any of it from

being the truth. I'd rather spend my life fighting with you than doing anything else."

She wiped at the tears in her eyes. "That was charmingly awful."

He rose to his feet but kept his grip on her elbows. "What? I'm telling you nothing matters if I don't have you, and you call it awful." He drew her closer, grazing his lips across her brow, over her eyelids, the tip of her nose. The touch of his lips, the gentle puff of his breath at odds with the growl of his words. Then finally, he claimed her mouth in a sweet, tender kiss.

When he pulled back, her eyes were teary. One of her curls wrapped itself around his finger. He rubbed his thumb against the strands before sliding his fingertips along her jaw, coaxing her.

"Say yes."

She stared into his intense gaze. "Yes. I love you, too."

"Will you ever do what I specifically ask you to do?"

"I will next time, if you ask nicely." Then she wrapped her arms around him and held on, knowing it would be for a lifetime.

Epilogue

"**W**hy can't I get ready in the master suite?" Gina moved out of Abby's reach and the hairpin she was holding in her hand. Her veil wasn't going anywhere, thanks to the dozen or more pins Abby had already jabbed into her scalp. She would be lucky not to need stitches from all the holes in her head.

"The light's better up here." Abby dusted Gina's nose with a sprinkle of powder.

"No, it's not. We added a window seat beneath the bay window in the corner. It catches the setting sun."

Abby and Katherine exchanged a look. Gigi stepped up and draped a strand of tiny pearls around Gina's neck, securing them underneath the fall of curls brushing the top of her shoulders.

Gina's stomach clenched when a glance in the mirror showed a shimmer in her grandmother's eyes. "What is it?" A horrible thought—no, fear—slammed into her. She whirled to face her mother, grandmother and two best friends. "If Toby's chickened out, you had better tell me now. Do not force me to become tomorrow's murderous headline."

"It—it isn't anything like that. It's just..." Abby glanced at Gina's mother.

But Katherine's stark logic beat out any placating attempts at excuses by the others. "Oh, go ahead and tell her. It isn't as if she'll be able to miss it when she lines up to walk down the aisle. And we all know how she hates not knowing something."

Abby and her mother nodded. "Okay. Toby and Mr. Tobias have a wedding present for you—"

Gina bunched her gown in her hands and headed for the door. "Oh, he's so wonderful." She glanced back at all four women. "Isn't he?"

Gigi, who had taken on her role as matron of honor with more vigor than a woman half her age could exhibit, shook her head. "Yes, dear, he's perfect. Now come back in here so we can finish getting you ready. You don't want to give him a chance to make a break for it."

"Gigi," Gina gasped. "Don't you think Toby wants to marry me?"

"Oh, he's desperate to marry you. He claimed in yesterday's paper that he couldn't wrap his head around any other stories for the paper without thoughts of you distracting him from his new job as managing editor."

Gina turned to Abby. "Do I need to remind him

your father was taking a big chance when he made him managing editor?"

Abby shrugged. "As the board of directors, Daddy, Judge Pierce and Nick agreed Toby would be the most conscientious editor they could find considering all the trouble Ivan caused the paper and him specifically."

Just then, a firm knock sounded at the door. Katherine rose from the love seat where she'd been sitting with her feet propped up, trying to stop her ankles from swelling. She fluffed the cascading ruffles of her knee-length ice-blue dress on her way to the door. "I'm so glad you picked this style dress. Nick was so tired of watching me strike different poses in front of the mirror, searching for the one that would mask the I-swallowed-a-watermelon look in your pictures."

"Oh, please." Gina rolled her eyes. "I look like the meringue off the top of a lemon meringue pie with all this fluff. You glow with impending motherhood."

Nick spoke softly to Katherine at the door. She nodded, and then opened it wider.

He held out his arm to her and Abby. "Ladies, I believe I'm your escort."

He led them from the room. Mr. Tobias, or Pops, as Toby wanted her to start calling his grandfather, handed Gigi a single white rose before offering her his arm. "Why don't we go do a little practice stroll for when it's your turn to take that walk toward me this summer?"

Gigi tittered and blushed like a young girl, then came to Gina. She clasped Gina's face in her hands and kissed both cheeks. "I'm so happy for you. Toby is a fine young man. He'll be a strong match for you, as you'll be for him."

Gina and her mother were the only ones left in the room. All the ladies of the wedding party were in ice-blue dresses the color of Toby's eyes. Her flowers were silk hydrangeas in shades of blue and white, with silver ribbons laced through them.

Her father came in to escort her down the stairs. He hugged her and her mom close. "My two beautiful girls."

Mia had wanted to help Frannie with the food as her gift. Frannie had insisted on catering everything, including the amazing cake that was covered in hand-scripted newsprint, recounting Toby's proposal and their wedding date.

The rest of her family had accepted Toby as easily as they had Pops. Expanding their clan and increasing the number of people to hug and love on at family gatherings. Toby didn't hold himself apart as if he thought he should stay on the fringes. He dove in, teasing her sisters, siding with her brothers and hugging Gigi and her mom with warmth and love.

Her family had blessed the house he'd reclaimed from his parents. Their efforts had helped turn it into the home of Toby's youth. Gary had made custom bookcases to hold Toby's professional awards and the snapshots that would document their lives in what would be Toby's home office. Gigi and Frannie had spent weeks tweaking the gourmet kitchen layout to the point that Gina and Toby had signed up for cooking classes just to consider themselves worthy of using the state-of-the-art appliances.

And Toby had a big surprise for her today aside

from his warmth and loving tenderness these past
weeks as they'd scoured antiques shops and estate
sales to furnish their house, looking for pieces that
showed the gentle wear of love.

For the past week, he and Pops had spent hours
secreted in the workshop behind the garage, sawing
and hammering, while she'd been banned from any
room along the back of the house where she might
get a peek out a window at what they were doing.
Her siblings had been more than happy to police her
time in the house, in case she tried to venture into a
cordoned-off area that might reveal the big secret.

And now here he stood, his hair cut short, his
black bow tie straight, his black jacket fitted across
his shoulders, his tuxedo pants creased sharp and his
crisp white shirt reflecting the last rays of the evening
sun. He waited for her in a redwood pergola, which
was woven with strands of flowering vines and twin-
kling lights. His wedding gift to her.

Jeremy stood all official and auspicious in his
black marrying-and-burying suit, as he referred to
it when Abby wasn't within earshot, already grinning his blessing for their union. Pops stood beside
Toby as his best man. And across the white carpeted
path strewn with silk rose petals stood Gigi, Abby
and Katherine.

The music began and her father led her down the
aisle in the slow, flowing pace they'd practiced yesterday. Her mother wiped her eyes as they made their
way closer to the procession flanking the white path
leading to the man God had chosen just for her. And
seeing the dimple of his smile as he mouthed the
words, "I love you," just before her father placed her

hand in his, Gina knew what they were starting today would last them a lifetime. Their love was making a house into a home and their union into a family filled with heaven's blessings. Forever.

* * * * *

REQUEST YOUR FREE BOOKS!

2 FREE INSPIRATIONAL NOVELS
PLUS 2
FREE
MYSTERY GIFTS

Love Inspired®

YES! Please send me 2 FREE Love Inspired® novels and my 2 FREE mystery gifts (gifts are worth about $10). After receiving them, if I don't wish to receive any more books, I can return the shipping statement marked "cancel." If I don't cancel, I will receive 6 brand-new novels every month and be billed just $4.99 per book in the U.S. or $5.49 per book in Canada. That's a saving of at least 17% off the cover price. It's quite a bargain! Shipping and handling is just 50¢ per book in the U.S. and 75¢ per book in Canada.* I understand that accepting the 2 free books and gifts places me under no obligation to buy anything. I can always return a shipment and cancel at any time. Even if I never buy another book, the two free books and gifts are mine to keep forever.

105/305 IDN GH5P

Name _____ (PLEASE PRINT)

Address _____ Apt. #

City _____ State/Prov. _____ Zip/Postal Code

Signature (if under 18, a parent or guardian must sign)

Mail to the **Reader Service:**
IN U.S.A.: P.O. Box 1867, Buffalo, NY 14240-1867
IN CANADA: P.O. Box 609, Fort Erie, Ontario L2A 5X3

**Are you a subscriber to Love Inspired® books
and want to receive the larger-print edition?
Call 1-800-873-8635 or visit www.ReaderService.com.**

* Terms and prices subject to change without notice. Prices do not include applicable taxes. Sales tax applicable in N.Y. Canadian residents will be charged applicable taxes. Offer not valid in Quebec. This offer is limited to one order per household. Not valid for current subscribers to Love Inspired books. All orders subject to credit approval. Credit or debit balances in a customer's account(s) may be offset by any other outstanding balance owed by or to the customer. Please allow 4 to 6 weeks for delivery. Offer available while quantities last.

Your Privacy—The Reader Service is committed to protecting your privacy. Our Privacy Policy is available online at www.ReaderService.com or upon request from the Reader Service.

We make a portion of our mailing list available to reputable third parties that offer products we believe may interest you. If you prefer that we not exchange your name with third parties, or if you wish to clarify or modify your communication preferences, please visit us at www.ReaderService.com/consumerchoice or write to us at Reader Service Preference Service, P.O. Box 9062, Buffalo, NY 14240-9062. Include your complete name and address.

LI15

REQUEST YOUR FREE BOOKS!

2 FREE INSPIRATIONAL NOVELS
PLUS 2 *FREE* MYSTERY GIFTS

Love Inspired® HISTORICAL

YES! Please send me 2 FREE Love Inspired® Historical novels and my 2 FREE mystery gifts (gifts are worth about $10). After receiving them, if I don't wish to receive any more books, I can return the shipping statement marked "cancel." If I don't cancel, I will receive 4 brand-new novels every month and be billed just $4.99 per book in the U.S. or $5.49 per book in Canada. That's a saving of at least 17% off the cover price. It's quite a bargain! Shipping and handling is just 50¢ per book in the U.S. and 75¢ per book in Canada.* I understand that accepting the 2 free books and gifts places me under no obligation to buy anything. I can always return a shipment and cancel at any time. Even if I never buy another book, the two free books and gifts are mine to keep forever.

102/302 IDN GH6Z

Name	(PLEASE PRINT)	

Address		Apt. #

City	State/Prov.	Zip/Postal Code

Signature (if under 18, a parent or guardian must sign)

Mail to the **Reader Service:**
IN U.S.A.: P.O. Box 1867, Buffalo, NY 14240-1867
IN CANADA: P.O. Box 609, Fort Erie, Ontario L2A 5X3

Want to try two free books from another series!
Call 1-800-873-8635 or visit www.ReaderService.com.

* Terms and prices subject to change without notice. Prices do not include applicable taxes. Sales tax applicable in N.Y. Canadian residents will be charged applicable taxes. Offer not valid in Quebec. This offer is limited to one order per household. Not valid for current subscribers to Love Inspired Historical books. All orders subject to credit approval. Credit or debit balances in a customer's account(s) may be offset by any other outstanding balance owed by or to the customer. Please allow 4 to 6 weeks for delivery. Offer available while quantities last.

Your Privacy—The Reader Service is committed to protecting your privacy. Our Privacy Policy is available online at www.ReaderService.com or upon request from the Reader Service.

We make a portion of our mailing list available to reputable third parties that offer products we believe may interest you. If you prefer that we not exchange your name with third parties, or if you wish to clarify or modify your communication preferences, please visit us at www.ReaderService.com/consumerchoice or write to us at Reader Service Preference Service, P.O. Box 9062, Buffalo, NY 14240-9062. Include your complete name and address.

LIH15